Fast Forward Japan

Stories by the Founding Father of
Japanese Science Fiction

Juza Unno

Translated by J.D. Wisgo

Arigatai Books

Published by Arigatai Books

For questions or comments about this book,
please contact the publisher via
arigataibooks@gmail.com

Please see https://www.arigataibooks.com for more
information on our books.

Edition: 1.01

ISBN: 978-1-7373182-1-7

"Humanity basks in the benefits of science, yet is haunted by its nightmares. We are enthralled by science, its opposing faces of good and evil, its blessings and curses. In this Age of Science, can we truly afford to not have science fiction?"

—Engraving on the Juza Unno Literary Monument in Tokushima Central Park, Japan

JUZA UNNO

CONTENTS

ACKNOWLEDGMENTS

Thanks to Kaimai Mizuhiro for helping confirm the meaning of the original Japanese text in a few places. Thanks to M. McCarn for helping with translation quality check, as well as Jim Miles, Cheryl Bhatnagar, Patrick Han, M. McCarn, and Akylina Printziou for helping with proofreading at some stage of this project.

FOUR-DIMENSIONAL MAN

For anyone who finds the personal account I am about to relate absurd, I encourage you to immediately stop and read no further; it would serve you better to flip through this book and read another author's masterfully written story. Because if you're the type of person who enjoys those addictive tales that seem real, but could never be—like being kissed on the streets of Ginza by a curly-haired girl, or suddenly whipping out a long *wakizashi* to cut down a crowd of 17 people—then you won't be able to appreciate the story I am about to tell, a story that seems impossible but did in fact happen. (I was going to express this in harsher terms, but as this is still the introduction I'll refrain.)

Well then, considering that the readers who have made it this far are, nine times out of ten, elite readers of a select group that will truly understand my feelings, perhaps it's time to calm down and begin the story proper—although I still can't let my guard down.

Now to return to the matter at hand. In the last year or two I've become aware of a certain oddity of my body. I am referring to the rare, unusual phenomenon whereby my body sometimes becomes invisible to others. Simply put, it seems to disappear without a trace, like a ghost.

How absurd, some readers will think. To all those readers, I request you do yourself a favor and refrain from reading any further. Otherwise, you'll become sick to your stomach, because the absurdity is only going to get thousands of times worse. Stop here for your own good.

Well then, remaining esteemed readers, you've done an admirable job reaching this point and maintaining calm.

You can only be described as *the cream of the crop*. I'd like to make a record of each of your honorable names, but as I write this I can hear someone say, "Enough buttering us up, get on with it already!" Alright, I understand. I will not get upset over any comments from my superior readers.

And so, I would like to address this to all my beloved readers that remain (though I still can't be too careful).

So you see, in the last year or two, I've become aware of a certain *oddity* of my body. On occasion, my body will curiously become completely invisible to others.

It is my belief that this mysterious phenomenon is not limited to me and there are others among the populace who share my experience. Perhaps being much wiser or more reserved than me, they can pose as normal members of society without revealing their secret. Those who maintain some sense of normalcy in their lives are surely trying to avoid being labeled as monsters and attracting attention, thereby ruining their chances to find a wonderful husband or wife from a well-respected family. However, in contrast to those more sensible folks, it so happens that I am by nature indifferent to such things and will express myself candidly on all matters, without the slightest reservation.

But it is my intention to give a detailed account of my own experiences here without concern for the business of others. I'd like to begin with the terrifying memory of when I first witnessed the *disappearance phenomenon* of my body.

I just said "terrifying memory," but on the surface the incident was far from terrifying. It happened two summers ago, when I had come home from work and washed a day's worth of sweat off in the foul-smelling water of my apartment's communal bath. Feeling refreshed, I slipped on a well-starched yukata and went out to wander the bustling evening streets of Shinjuku. For whatever reason, human beings tend to do the most irrational things. That is of little interest to me, but anyway, I browsed through the numerous night stalls as I made the rounds of each and every shady side street, watched a short documentary and a theatre performance, and finally ended up drinking a cup of black coffee that has been in short supply lately, savoring the flavor sip by sip with deliberate movements, like a video captured with a high-speed camera. Even though the needle of the clock read 10 p.m., when I went outside not even a single person remained on the once-bustling streets—well, while not strictly true, this is an apt description of the desolation there—leading me to believe the actual time was a good deal past midnight. (Mind you, that clock had been digital. To readers who doubt there was a shop where you can drink black coffee until after midnight, I'd like to inform you of the existence of underground coffee shops. If you don't believe me, consider it useless to read further as you will surely not believe the true account I am about to tell.)

Due to the gradual weeding out of readers, I feel that the time has finally come to begin the central part of my tale. I had just set forth down a sparsely populated sidewalk. My apartment was in Totsuka 3-chome, so when coming from Shinjuku the fastest shortcut took me across a lonely part of Toyama fields. On that day I followed my usual routine and took the same route, but this put me on a direct collision course with a terrible discovery.

Methodically extinguishing every single streetlight as I went, I walked by a certain department store that looked like a giant cardboard box tossed onto the street, and then shuffled through a sleepy retail district bearing a resemblance to an uneven, poorly made wall, when I finally approached the entrance to the Toyama fields.

Oh, the Toyama fields at night!

What a truly peaceful place, known to only a select few. Sawtooth oaks covered the entire region, tranquil as an untouched forest, and there were no trash piles, sewer planks, or abandoned handcarts, to say nothing of marquees or neon signs. What was there was mostly dirt, along with oak trees, short weeds, empty boxes of caramel candy, and papers rustling along the ground. It was a truly desolate field; if this was a Kabuki performance I'd play some traditional *ozatsuma* music, drop a pale blue curtain to the sound of a wooden clapper, and loudly ring a *honzuri* bell, but unfortunately I had none of those things prepared—

leaving only the sound of bugs buzzing in the grass just as the moon broke through the clouds, the silky light flowing like water, and the oak trees focused a faint image of their trunks onto my eyes. Or more simply: the moon came out and the forest got brighter.

Just then, I was shocked to see someone here in Toyama fields, which I had been certain was an uninhabited place. A few people had suddenly emerged from the woods. There were two: a young man and a woman.

They chatted animatedly together as they approached me. Seeing them somehow irritated me, but I'm sure you understand how I felt. To spite them, I purposefully walked in the direction where I would get in their way. I expected the young couple to immediately detect my ill intent and evade sideways. However, no matter how close I got, they made no attempt to evade. This angered me, compounding my irritation.

If I continued on forward like this, I would have no choice but to run into them. The couple headed directly towards me, their course unchanged. I considered swerving to avoid them. But then it dawned on me: *there was absolutely no reason for me to avoid them.* Those two were thoroughly enjoying themselves; I was alone and not enjoying myself in the slightest. Given that, was it so unreasonable for a lucky couple to yield to unlucky me?

I squinted and charged headlong towards them.

Watch out!

My body struck the young man with a thud.

"Ouch!" he cried out and staggered backward. *He's going to fall, poor thing,* I thought, but I was mistaken; the young man firmly planted a foot on the ground and regained his balance.

"Oh, that's weird," muttered the young man. "But like I was saying, I told my uncle, 'If this doesn't work out...' "

"Hey, what just happened? You nearly fell over," said the young woman.

"Yeah, I suddenly lost my balance for some reason. But it didn't hurt or anything...So I told my uncle—"

11

"But that was really weird. It looked like you suddenly got dizzy."

"Come on, it's no big deal. You know I've been a little stressed out lately..."

The young couple conversed as they left, leaving me there speechless.

For a while, I sat in the grassy field, watching them walk away.

Those two are quite careless...or simply insensitive. They're really something! They were so absorbed in their conversation that they didn't realize I had knocked into them.

But wait a minute. Something still doesn't seem right. It's strange they didn't see me standing right in front of them. Very strange.

I continued through the oak forest, the strange feeling lingering. The grass at my feet glittered in the moonlight streaming down through the treetops.

Just then, I spotted another couple tiptoeing out of the forest.

Indeed, this is a night of many couples!

The depression that fell over me soon became resentment.

I might as well also slam into these two!

My impure urge became harder and harder to suppress, until at last I dashed forward towards where they stood close together and collided with them. And what do you think happened?

I was more surprised than they were, as you can guess from the following exchange.

"Hey, stop that, Matsushima!"

"Huh? What's wrong with you? You're the one who bumped into..."

Each of them believed the other had done it. There was no indication they were aware of me, now standing behind them after slipping between their bodies.

Seeing this, I too couldn't help but mutter, "Well, this is odd!"

"Hey...Somebody else is here."

"No, there's nobody here."

"Oh, I guess you're right. But I could have sworn I heard someone say 'this is odd' or something like that..."

They were facing me during this exchange; not to mention they didn't seem to have even realized I was there.

At that moment I felt a tingle run along the back of my neck, a terrible sensation I still remember to this day.

How Strange...It was like nobody noticed me. Not those two from earlier, nor this couple. How can that be possible?

A strange feeling gradually overcame me. My heart danced in my chest. I think I was on the verge of losing my mind.

I felt guilty, and at the same time terrified, yet I tried it again with the third couple. Once more the outcome was truly regrettable. No one seemed to realize I existed; my body was invisible to them. How can such a regrettable, terrifying thing like this happen again?

I spent over an hour laying on the grass in Toyama fields, alone in anguish. During that time the clouds obscured the moon, darkening everything in the vicinity, so I stood up and returned to my apartment. I unlocked the door, entered my room, and climbed into bed. I slept until morning.

A carefree person by nature, I soon forgot about the terrifying events of the previous night, and when I woke up I headed to the bathroom, toothbrush and towel in hand.

"Hey, are you getting up now? Slept pretty late, huh," a voice said to me.

I was startled; the voice was Dr. Fujita's, a street face reader rumored to be a resident of this apartment since its construction.

I didn't respond.

"What's with that face? You look like a distressed rat stuck under a *kagami-mochi* rice cake."

Dr. Fujita, being his usual self, volleyed a harsh remark at me. I struggled hard to keep myself from asking the burning question: *Dr. Fujita, can you see me now?* I turned around to look behind me. I wanted to check if Dr. Fujita's remark was aimed at another person standing behind me.

After everything that had happened, I was immensely relieved by what I saw: nobody was behind me. I could see through clearly to the end of the hallway. No one was there, not even a cat.

"Hey, Dr. Fujita. It seems like you're in a good mood, I guess you made some money last night," I said, laughing for the first time in a while.

"That wasn't the first time!" Fujita said with a giggle. "It appears that my greedy customers have been well off these days, leaving me a tip on top of my usual fee. Extraordinary times!" He chuckled loudly.

Fujita's laugh was priceless, for it told me my body was undeniably visible. Thanks to Dr. Fujita, this was proven without a doubt. I was so happy I could die and go to heaven.

The joy! The relief!

However, I still had no explanation for that night's strange occurrences at Toyama fields. Why had I been invisible to them on that particular night?

I discussed this with my good friend Shiraishi. However, I presented it not as my own personal experience, but as that of a third person.

Whereupon Shiraishi sneered at me and said, "Well that's obvious. The assumption that his body (actually my body) wasn't visible is plain wrong."

"What do you mean?"

"In other words, from the perspective of those young couples meeting in secret at a place like that, a random man who suddenly bumps into them is a strange, frightening figure, so in keeping with the expression 'let sleeping dogs lie' they simply pretended to not see him. They knew that angering him would only make matters worse and cause them a great deal of trouble."

"Hmm, I see. It's that simple," I laughed.

"What's so funny? You're a strange guy."

Shiraishi stared suspiciously at me, but I couldn't have been happier.

Unfortunately, my happiness didn't last even five days. One night, on the way home from Shinjuku as I entered

Toyama fields, the same thing happened. Once again, my existence was utterly ignored.

My sorrow could be likened to the recurrence of a terrible sickness. Shiraishi's words had kept me happy for only a little under three days. I was plunging headfirst, yet again, into an infinite hell of darkness. What was happening to me? To think a person's body could become completely invisible...

There didn't seem to be any deception on their part. When someone couldn't see me, they really couldn't see me. This terrified me, but at the same time aroused a secret curiosity about why this was happening. However, the answer was not quick in coming.

I had no desire to tell my accursed tale to anyone else. Had I done that, a circus promoter would soon be after me, trying to make me into an exhibit: *Hurry, step right up and take a look! Only pay if you like what you see!*

I just wanted to be normal.

Having said that, I couldn't just sit around doing nothing with this mystery left unsolved, so I troubled Dr. Fujita to read my fortune. I thought perhaps he would discover something unusual in my facial structure.

Using a magnifying glass that rendered my wrinkles as large as the Sumida River, Dr. Fujita gazed at my face long and hard enough to dig a hole through it. Suddenly a look of surprise appeared on his face and he drew back, as if in fear. When he began to speak there was a certain formality in his voice.

"Hmm, this is the first time I've seen your face up close like this, but I must say you have extremely unique *features*. I was quite shocked."

"What do you mean by 'unique features'?" I asked, beginning to feel uncomfortable.

Dr. Fujita, in a departure from his usual laziness, placed his hands firmly on his knees.

"Legend has it that once, long ago, one of my senior colleagues did a face reading for the servant Tokichiro Kinoshita and foretold he would rule over the land. But my colleague was so surprised by his own prediction and shocked that fortune telling was quackery, he broke his divining sticks there on the spot, threw them into the river, and declared he was giving up the profession, but after all that Tokichiro Kinoshita went on to become Toyotomi Hideyoshi. Nonetheless, at this very moment I'm considering selling off my magnifying glass and mystical fortune-telling books to a pawn shop."

"Hey, don't try to threaten me. What in the world are you talking about..."

"Your face. It has a rare combination of features only found once in a quadrillion, if that. If my reading is correct, you are not an inhabitant of this reality we are experiencing now."

"Wait, what did you just say? I'm not understanding at all."

"Nothing is beyond your understanding. You, my friend, are an *ultraterrestrial*."

"Ultraterrestrial? I'm even more confused now. I may be an ultraterrestrial, but I'm standing before you now in the body of a respectable Japanese person."

In the wake of my arrogant declaration came a disturbing revelation, triggered by the recall of those terrifying events. I shuddered as the memory of that night in the Toyama fields, when my body had apparently become invisible, came back to me.

Dr. Fujita ignored me and continued.

"To put it simply, what I see of you with my eyes now is nothing but a slice of your true form taken from a certain angle. Let's say I have a daikon radish. If I were to cut it somewhere in the middle, you would only see the ellipse-shaped surface of the slice. You would think, 'Oh, that's a juicy, pure white ellipse-shaped surface.' But that white surface is nothing but a single slice of the radish. There is more to the radish than that surface. Similarly, what I see of you now, standing before me, is nothing but a single slice of your true form. Your true form, like the radish for which only a white slice was visible, is something that transcends our imagination."

"I'm not following you."

"But at least theoretically, you understand me, right? Now consider this. In our world, everything has height, width, and depth. Basically, three dimensions."

"Right, our world is three-dimensional."

"But now assume that our world has only two dimensions. There is height and width, but no depth. A world like the surface of calm water. A world of a geometrical plane."

"Ok, so a two-dimensional world."

"So now let's say we slowly dip that radish into the water. At first, only its tip breaches the water's surface. At that point, in the two-dimensional world the radish is only visible as a tiny point."

"Sure."

"However, as I plunge the radish deeper into the water, the portion crossing the water's surface gradually expands to a white circle. In the two-dimensional world, the point seems to gradually grow to become a white circle. But once the leafy part finally reaches the water, what appeared until now as a white circle suddenly transforms into a scattering of several green bands. These bands are continually moving, changing shape. Finally, when the topmost part of the leaves submerges below the water's surface, in the two-dimensional world there is nothing left to be seen."

"I see. How strange."

"What began as a white point soon becomes a large white disc, then a scattering of green bands, until it finally disappears completely. This looks like a ghost to those life forms in the two-dimensional world, but to us, in the three-dimensional world it is essentially nothing more than a daikon radish penetrating the still surface of the water as it gradually submerges. However, two-dimensional life forms cannot even imagine the shape of the radish that we perceive. Those in the two-dimensional world have no facility to truly perceive three-dimensional objects."

"Wow, you're a pretty amazing scientist."

"That's right, face reading *is* science. But back to what I was saying. According to my reading, you are not a three-dimensional being, but rather a *four-dimensional* one. You might think such an absurd thing could never actually happen, but that's what the reading says, so I don't know what to tell you. Actually, I think I'm going to quit face reading, starting now. It's complete quackery."

My only response to this was to sigh repeatedly. I was deeply moved by Dr. Fujita's words. However, I lacked the energy to declare dramatically that I, like Tokichiro Kinoshita, would wildly succeed in life, and that Dr. Fuijta's reading was correct. I could only lament why I, of all people, had been born as a cursed human being—or should I say cursed life form. At the same time, a curiosity sparked in me about what my true form was, if I was in fact a four-dimensional being.

Since then, I've lived as a recluse. It seems that there are still times when my body becomes invisible to others. Occasionally, someone will unexpectedly bump into me, and each time I'll tell myself, *here we go again*.

I did some research the other day but could not find any information about who my parents were. So I knew I must have been adopted. That's why there's no way to know if I was actually born from a human womb. Nevertheless, there can't be a single person who has a clear memory of being born. The claim that someone came from their mother's womb is merely misinformation. Consequently, I suspect there may be a surprising number of people who are also four-dimensional beings like me, living carelessly without knowledge of their condition.

Those people must be extremely careful. Whenever someone bumps into you on the street or anywhere else, be sure to reflect on this, keeping in mind that you may be invisible to the other party—or perhaps even a cross section of a four-dimensional being.

THE WORLD IN ONE THOUSAND YEARS

Death by Freezing

Seven days had already passed since the young, ambitious scientist Dr. Furuhata awoke in his coffin.

"I wonder what's going on outside. Someone should have already been tapping on the coffin lid by now."

He waited eagerly, listening intently for the sound of a knock on his coffin.

The word "coffin" here doesn't refer to the plain wooden coffin that everyone is familiar with; it was a five-layer coffin made from the magnificent metal MO 902, a durable molybdenum alloy. The coffin's interior was considerably spacious—unlike those narrow wooden coffins with barely enough room to lay down—roughly the size of a 10-tatami room with a high ceiling. There was a bed, along with various pieces of equipment: a freezer, air conditioner, gas producer, electric generator, and signaling device. Many reference books were piled up inside, along with various necessities for daily life including an ashtray, toothbrush, and safety razor. Simply put, it resembled a study and research lab condensed into one.

Dr. Furuhata had already spent over 1,000 years in cryogenic sleep inside this odd-looking coffin.

Cryogenic sleep is the process of freezing a person alive and keeping them in that state for as many years as needed. This is an extremely difficult technique, in particular because of the speed at which freezing occurs. Done poorly, the subject stays dead for all eternity; done properly, the frozen human's life is preserved, whether that is three days later, 100 years later or—as in Dr. Furuhata's case—1,000 years later. If thawed with just the right timing, the subject can be brought back to life. The technique of thawing a frozen human also turns out to be extremely difficult, but in Dr. Furuhata's case, both of these went smoothly without a hitch.

This is to be expected; the experiment on this young scientist was not performed by his efforts alone, but rather in cooperation with a group of scientists with the lengthy name "1,000-Year Human Cryogenics Project Research Council."

As previously mentioned, inside the coffin was a square-shaped room, but on the outside it had a spherical shape designed to withstand force from any angle.

Seven days after awakening from his 1,000-year sleep, Dr. Furuhata had completely recovered from fatigue. It felt like only yesterday when he had first entered the coffin. Sleeping for a thousand years was an impressive feat.

But had he truly slept for a thousand years? The radium clock on the wall assured he had. Designed to measure radium's eternal radioactive decay, it kept track of the long span of time. The instant Dr. Furuhata woke up he rushed over to check the elapsed time. He had apparently overslept a tad beyond 1,000 years: the clock read the 169th day of the 1,000th year, equivalent to the winter of February 3600 in the common era. This meant the coffin's systems had introduced an error of 169 days. However, compared to 1,000 years, 169 days was an extremely tiny error. More importantly, during those 1,000 years Dr. Furuhata's life was preserved perfectly in a cryogenic state, so it's fair to say the caliber of those systems deserves high praise.

The bigger concern was that after 1,000 years, Dr. Furuhata had not heard anyone knocking outside the coffin, despite the pressing need for that. According to the coffin's specifications, in order to remain tightly sealed for 1,000 years it would only open from the outside. This was the only way to ensure structural integrity.

"What could have happened? Perhaps because I woke up 169 days late, the person who was going to open the door went traveling somewhere."

To someone locked in a room, being plagued by this kind of uncertainty was more terrifying than even the death penalty.

"The signaling device may be malfunctioning," he thought and walked up to it. Repeated inspections, however, didn't turn up any problems. If the device was functioning, his awakening should have been communicated over the airwaves to three cities: Tokyo, New York, and Khabarovsk.

"Why has nobody come for me?"

If no one came to open the door, Dr. Furuhata—finally awakened after all this time—would be able to survive a good 30 days, but after that there was little hope. He was not lamenting the loss of his life, but rather the misfortune of being brought back to life 1,000 years later, only to die without ever seeing the world.

Naked Professor Woman

That's when it happened.

Briiing. Briiing. Briiiiiiing.

The clear sound of the alarm bell resounded in the closed room, energizing the air within.

"Oh, someone's here! Someone's here! They're finally here! Someone is tapping on the coffin lid!"

The alarm bell was designed to ring whenever someone tapped on the coffin lid. "I'm saved!" thought Dr. Furuhata. An instant later, a massive tremor shook the room. The coffin was finally opening.

Once Dr. Furuhata's excitement abated, it was replaced by a great curiosity about who had come to open the coffin. This curiosity grew increasingly intense as the moment approached when the door of this enclosed space would be opened.

The door burst open and someone entered the coffin from the near darkness outside.

Dr. Furuhata let out an outrageously loud cry. It was a voice of utter surprise: the first visitor he laid his eyes on after being revived was completely naked. Literally naked in every sense of the word. To make matters worse, in a glance it was clear that the visitor was a young woman. Dr. Furuhata's face flushed bright red with embarrassment. The woman, on the other hand, instead of blushing stood there nonchalantly, as if nothing unusual had happened.

"Assistant Professor Furuhata, I presume?"

"Yes, I am Furuhata. Thank you for opening the door."

"It's my great pleasure to discover someone who lived 1,000 years ago. When I was destroying the 199th air defense partition, I found a record describing you inside of a long, stainless-steel pipe."

"Oh, I see," Dr. Furuhata said, remembering that long ago his friends had placed his burial record into 200 sturdy pipes, putting them on display at museums and burying them at various places throughout the world.

"So what would your name be?"

"My name? I am Chita, Head of Archaeology at Khabarovsk College."

"Wow, you're the Head of Archaeology!" Dr. Furuhata made no attempt to hide his surprise. "With all due respect, being the Head of Archaeology must be a challenge for someone as young as you."

Chita laughed. "Who said I was young? I'm having my 903rd birthday this year!"

"Seriously? So you'll be 903 years old. That's incredible!"

With the athletic legs of a 19- or 20-year-old, it was hard to believe she was actually 903 years old. Not to mention, was it even possible for someone to live that long?

She laughed again. "I'm so happy to hear you say that. Watching you standing there, I think I have some idea now of the intellectual level of mankind 1,000 years ago. How enlightening!" she said, openly enjoying herself. "But I shouldn't be the only one enjoying myself here. Let me tell you about the world now, 1,000 years later."

Caressing her blond hair, Professor Chita explained how 900 years ago mankind had conquered death itself.

Essentially, humans no longer needed to die. What a monumental discovery!

When Dr. Furuhata asked how that happened, she went on to describe how all medical conditions were now diagnosable through the science of electricity and curable via electrotherapy, thanks to advances in understanding human physiology. People with failing hearts could now easily replace them with artificial ones. Those with high blood pressure could completely replace their blood vessels in a half-days' time. As a result, no one had to die who didn't want to.

Even so, at the time these amazing medical advances occurred artificial organs were extremely expensive and because of their metal construction exceedingly heavy, rendering patients unable to walk.

Initially, replacing three organs—heart, lungs, and kidney—tripled that person's total weight, making walking unassisted impossible. When traveling around a city there was no choice but to ride in a vehicle the entire time.

But now things were different. People with artificial organs could freely walk around. The organs had become lightweight from a combination of small size and pressure-resistant artificial tissue instead of metal.

"Behold the result of all this: my body," Professor Chita said. "There's nothing unnatural about it. And look how easily I can move it around."

Standing before Dr. Furuhata, she flaunted her legs adeptly like a revue girl.

In the face of yet another surprise, Dr. Furuhata could only stare wide-eyed at the woman.

"So, basically a 903-year-old woman like you is able to live that long due to artificial organs?"

"Yes, of course."

"Wow, that's really surprising. From here I can't tell at all where your artificial organs are. I guess it's because they've become so small and light. But there's one odd thing. Professor Chita, are you sure you aren't joking with me?"

"Why would you say such a thing? I'm being completely honest with you."

"But don't you think it's odd? If you actually installed artificial organs in your body, then there must be some scars from the surgery somewhere, like on your chest or lower abdomen. However, the body I see before me is as beautiful as that of a 19- or 20-year-old girl. There aren't even any small scars from stitches. Don't you think that is incredibly odd?"

Hearing that, Professor Chita grinned as if she pitied Dr. Furuhata's aged brain.

"Dr. Furuhata, 950 years ago the field of surgery was perfected and scars are no longer needed. However, my body is not free of scars thanks to that ancient technology. It's free of scars thanks to artificial skin."

"What is *artificial skin*?"

"It's a substance similar to artificial tissue. Since it's artificial, I can just tear it off at any time and put on a new one."

"Oh...I see," Dr. Furuhata mumbled, but he was astounded. He had been staring red-faced at Professor Chita's stark-naked body, but if that was artificial skin then there was nothing to be embarrassed about.

"So that means—and I'm sorry if I'm being rude—that your body is now considerably different than your real body that came from your mother's womb."

"Well, I guess that is mostly accurate."

"Then aren't your skeletal and facial structure the only things remaining from your original body?"

"No, not exactly."

"So there is something else left?"

"No, quite the contrary. Even the facial structure you speak of is completely different. To be honest, by nature I was not very good-looking, with a protruding forehead, recessed eyes, large mouth, and a curved nose. That's why I had my face completely replaced. I just looked through the face catalog and had my face fixed to match the one I liked the best. Nothing has troubled ancient humanity as much as aesthetics of the face. Come to think of it, humans back then were terribly ignorant. The beauty of a face is determined by the shape and arrangement of the well-known elements that constitute it: eyes, eyebrows, nose, lips, and teeth. If the eyes are recessed, simply implant some tissue there. That type of surgery is trivial. Once artificial skin and tissue were invented, ugly people started fixing their faces in droves, becoming attractive men and women. Let's head out to the city now. I'm certain you won't find a single ugly man or woman out there."

"Oh..." Lost for words, this was all Dr. Furuhata could say. He believed beauty had held sway over humanity for the last 30,000 years, so when he discovered faces could now be changed freely, he could only sigh in wonder.

War with Mars

At last, the time had come for Dr. Furuhata to step foot outside the coffin. It was overwhelming to think that this would be his first time walking upon the earth in over 1,000 years.

He stepped outside and found what appeared to be a partially dug tunnel. On the ground nearby lay an object resembling a water gun.

"What is this?" Dr. Furuhata asked.

"A device for digging holes. It can easily make holes in earth, concrete, or steel. I just dug that cave out myself with it in a little over 30 minutes," Professor Chita said.

At first, he thought such an unbelievable thing could not be true. But once the professor explained that the device used a massive discharge of energy from atomic decay, it made more sense.

"So, I guess all power now is generated by extracting energy from atomic decay."

The professor answered in the affirmative, her face betraying annoyance from being asked about such an ancient thing.

When they stepped foot outside the cave, they were greeted with a cityscape identical to a picture once published in a science magazine titled *The World in 10 Million Years*. The sprawl of hundreds of roads running in all possible directions was a remarkable sight. Unlike those Dr. Furuhata knew, never once did this swarm of roads cross itself. They were staggered vertically with nothing akin to traditional intersections, so there was no stopping for traffic lights, no matter how far you went.

Even more surprising was the lack of a car or any other vehicles on the roads. The people upon them whooshed by like bullets, moving at incredible speeds.

"Those people out there sure are running quickly."

Professor Chita laughed at Dr. Furuhata when he sighed like a man from the country.

"No, Dr. Furuhata. Those people are not running, the road itself is moving. I've heard that roads long ago were stationary and things like cars and trains moved above them. You see, modern roads all move at a rapid pace. If someone steps foot upon one, they can be transported to wherever they desire."

"A moving road...what an amazing mechanism! The calculations are immense, even just considering power, and the resources required are..."

Professor Chita interrupted Dr. Furuhata mid-sentence. "In this day and age, energy is unlimited. By breaking down matter we can extract as much energy as we want, a massive amount of energy incomparable to ancient times. There's nothing to be concerned about."

Dr. Furuhata was in awe; the world had become a place where power was no longer a concern. Humanity had entered a truly fortunate age.

Just then, Dr. Furuhata thought of something important to ask Professor Chita.

"Hey, Professor Chita. In modern times, are there still wars?"

"Wars? Yes, of course there are wars."

A voice suddenly bellowed out from somewhere nearby and echoed throughout the city. Someone was clamoring about something. Professor Chita's face stiffened a little.

When the noise died down, Dr. Furuhata asked, "What was that? I guess that loud voice came from a speaker."

"That's correct. It was an announcement from the Emigration Headquarters, asking for all people up to a certain number to ascend to the surface and gather before the emigration rocket."

"So...this is not the surface?"

"No, of course not. This is 500 meters below the surface."

"Oh, then we're in an underground city. Professor Chita, I would like to see the surface. I'm very eager to find out how it has changed."

"Absolutely not," the professor said, flatly rejecting Dr. Furuhata's request. "Those who have not been instructed to cannot go to the surface. Emigration is by order only, that's why they are able to go above like that."

"Emigration? Where are they emigrating to?"

"They're going to Venus. People are being periodically sent to Venus in large numbers."

"Venus...You mean that Venus?" Furuhata was shocked. "At last, the day has come when we travel to the stars..."

"If things go well, in another three months all humans from Earth will be transferred to Venus."

"Really? So the Earth will be empty? Why are we abandoning our precious Earth?"

"We've discovered that in about a year, the Earth will be smashed to bits when it collides with the X comet."

"Oh, I see. So the Earth is going to collide with a comet," Dr. Furuhata nodded. "That's why there's a need to emigrate from Earth. But then why don't we instead go to Mars, whose climate is closest to Earth?"

Professor Chita looked back at Dr. Furuhata and spoke, her face uncharacteristically grim.

"Your lack of intelligence befits your age. At present, humans on Earth are at war with Martian life forms. The instant we decided to emigrate to Venus, the Martian interference began. To date, only 7% percent of the rockets have arrived safely on Mars, with the remaining 93% destroyed by the Martians, those inside brutally murdered. It's only natural; after all, the Martians are far more devious than us. You know, I think humanity should have begun preparations for space warfare at a much earlier stage. Our presumption that we were the most intelligent form of life in this vast universe was the ultimate form of hubris."

Upon hearing this, Dr. Furuhata finally understood that this war in space was what Professor Chita had meant by "of course we have wars."

THE THEORY OF PLANETARY COLONIZATION

"**M**r. Editor, before I leave, is there anything else you want me to ask him?"

"No, I don't think so. Just remember you're interviewing a well-known figure, considered eccentric even in academic circles, so use your looks and usual charm to find some way to bring me back a great article. If things go well, I might get you that roadster you've been wanting for so long."

"Well then, it's a promise! If you buy me a roadster, I'll be able to marry my darling six months earlier. I'm so happy!"

"Alright, save your celebrating for later. Now hurry up and go get that story! The taxi fare is fifty sen."

"Excuse me, what floor is Professor Gorgonzola's research lab?"

"That would be the thirty-eighth floor!"

"To there please."

"Alright everyone, going up. Please notify me promptly of the floor you would like to get off. Anyone for the second floor? Makeup, shoes, bags, and neckties. Third floor, cotton wear. Anyone getting off here? Next is the fourth floor, silk products, *meisen* and *habutae* silk. Fifth floor, cafeteria. Next is the sixth and seventh floors, and we will be skipping all subsequent floors until our last stop. Those who want to get off on an intermediate floor, please transfer to another elevator. Anyone? Alright, this is the thirty-eighth floor. Everyone off. Please check for forgotten items. Thank you for your patronage."

"Well now, this is the rooftop. There's certainly no professor's lab here. Oh wait, I see a nameplate over there. It looks like a stork's nest perched on top of the Eiffel Tower. Alright, I have to gather up the courage to climb that iron ladder for my darling waiting for me down below, but also for that roadster, for the article money, and for my editor. I hope people won't gather at the bottom of the ladder when I'm climbing up. Here we go!"

Knock knock.

"Professor Gorgonzola!"

" ..."

"Professor Gorgonzola! If you don't answer, I'll use wire cutters to cut your high voltage line! Is anybody home...?"

"Who dares to commit such recklessness?"

"Professor, I've brought a letter of invitation."

"Oh wow, aren't you a beauty! I don't need to see any letter of invitation. Come in, come in!"

"Oh my, until this moment I had not realized how powerful my sex appeal was. It's a great pleasure to meet you. By the way, your laboratory looks really odd. It's like you formed a room out of Euclidean shapes and then chrome plated it. Do you believe that the secrets of the universe can be solved with Euclidean geometry?"

"At small distances, yes."

"What kind of distances does your latest project involve?"

"Latest project?"

"You know what I'm talking about. It's the elephant in the room, your 'Theory of Interplanetary Colonization.' "

"Oh, so that's why you're here. Did you know there is one condition required for interplanetary colonization?"

"No professor, I didn't know that. What type of condition?"

"Nothing to worry, you'll come to understand in due time."

"OK, then we can talk about that later, professor. So what was your inspiration for the theory of interplanetary colonization?"

"The world we live in is such a tiny place. That's all."

"Are you saying that the world is tiny, even the country of Manchuria?"

"The population will increase until there is no room left on the planet. But that's not all. There's the wanderlust of our species. Our desire to have more. The psychology of skipping two or three train cars just to get on one that isn't packed. Are you following me? That's what will drive us to colonize other planets."

"Interesting. So you mean that planetary colonization will occur not out of necessity, but out of greed?"

"Precisely. Humans will try to satisfy any desire their ability permits. After achieving everything there is to achieve, they will develop that ability further and set their sights on a new desire. Their greed will never cease. Science is almighty, but at the same time it is not. Simply put, science is almighty in a relative sense, not in an absolute sense. Expressed in elementary mathematics, it would be correct to state that 'Science is almighty.' "

"Sorry, I'm not very good at philosophy."

"No, you aren't very good at advanced mathematics."

"In any case, how can planetary colonization be realized?"

"There are many ways to go about it. I can't describe them all now, but I'll tell you three or four that are easy for a layperson to understand. First, we can conquer the moon."

"Oh dear!"

"We can equip a rocket, a terribly fast aircraft shaped like a bullet, with a television broadcast system and fly it all around the moon, then study the moon's geography by watching a broadcast from its surface on a monitor located on Earth. This technique could also apply to the colonization of other planets."

"That sounds like aerial reconnaissance."

"Next, the landing site will be finalized, and plans made for how humans from Earth will survive after they land—things like food, clothing, and shelter. Once planning is complete, people on Earth will board a rocket and fly to the moon, touching down at the agreed-upon location."

"That seems like it would take a long time."

"Perhaps, but eventually it will only take a week."

"What will happen after that?"

"Energy acquisition is of foremost importance. Energy radiating from the sun can be captured and a power plant constructed. Heat and light are generated, and various goods manufactured using that energy. Over time, larger and larger goods can be produced until eventually the moon warms up from the large number of massive power plants, steam and water become easily available, and perhaps even breathable air has begun floating above the surface, resulting in conditions identical to those on Earth."

"I see. It seems like everything will go smoothly."

"As the Earth ages, immigration will begin to other planets close to the sun, such as Venus. Circumstances permitting, we can even bring Earth itself right up next to Venus."

"You can actually do that?"

"Indeed we can. All that is needed is to create a gravity cancellation device. Using a piezo crystal—nowadays we can make tiny ones, but soon larger ones will become available—we may be able to establish a free route for the Earth."

"And what would a 'free route' for the Earth be?"

"By 'free route,' I mean that Earth would no longer have to revolve in the same orbit around the sun. Just like steering a taxi, someday Earth may be able to move to wherever in the universe we desire."

"That's amazing!"

"On the way, those fed up with the Earth can freely migrate to nearby planets."

"But won't humans on the other planets get upset?"

"Yes, that is a concern. However, according to my theory, it is not likely to be a problem. First of all, over the last ten years scholars around the world have been researching radio waves from other planets, yet nothing even close to a signal has been discovered. This is proof that no one out there is calling out to Earth. On the other hand, here on Earth we have been transmitting constantly on shortwave, UHF, and VHF, sending signals which penetrate the Kennelly-Heaviside layer and scatter far into the universe. While they are intended to be received on Earth, these signals also leak outside the Earth's atmosphere. Just considering this, it is clear that us humans on Earth are the most advanced life form."

"Even I can understand that."

"Second, there is the fact that humans on Earth have never been invaded by a life form from another planet. Hypothetically, if we were to travel to another planet, we would go with the intention of killing any life there. And yet, on Earth we have not received even a single attack from another planet. This too indicates there are no lifeforms in the universe more advanced than us. Broadly speaking, we can say that humans are the lords of creation."

"Oh Professor, your intellect is truly astounding..."

"You see, young lady, we will be fine for the time being. But it's doubtful whether we will be able to maintain our position of dominance 20,000 years from now. By that time, a superior life form may exist on a planet somewhere and carry out a full-scale conquest of Earth."

"How unfortunate."

"If that happens, large-scale wars on Earth will surely stop. After all, we'll have to defend ourselves from the attacks of another planet. That's why it's best if Earth starts colonizing planets now that show promise, so if something happens we will be in a good position to fight back. Anyway, humans will be able to transform this vast universe into something like a paradise much quicker than you would expect. It may take only 20,000 years. However, if we get a head start on this project, we can achieve our objective one or two thousand years sooner."

"What do you mean by 'get a head start'?"

"Right now, in the entire world there are fifteen people thinking about sending a rocket to another planet, and of those, only two have actually constructed such a rocket."

"Wow, have things actually gotten that far? That's a surprise to me."

"Would you like to take a ride on one of those rockets?"

"I think I would, professor."

"Oh, really? Then take a look outside that window."

"Oh wow, professor. I see a panoramic view. It's like I am watching the Earth, the size of a soccer ball, from somewhere out there in the universe..."

"Look closely. The Earth is shrinking fast before your eyes!"

"Oh no, this is terrible...I feel so strange now..."

"Listen carefully. You can hear the rumble of the engine, right? There's also the sound of gas being propelled from the rocket."

"So that means..."

"This rocket is now 950,000 kilometers from Earth."

"Professor, stop kidding around. Please return me to Earth immediately!"

"I have been waiting for a beautiful young woman like you to enter this room."

"But professor, my fiancée is..."

"Launch preparations for my rocket had already been completed on that building's 38th floor. The only remaining element required for interplanetary colonization was the essential man-woman pair, which I am half of. With the arrival of my mate, everything was in place to launch. Well now, shall we search for a new planet in the Orion constellation? On our new planet, you will give birth to many children. You may not be happy now, but in 200,000 years things are going to get as lively as Earth. Yes, what a magnificent voyage we have before us!"

"Mr. Editor, oh how could you! And Earth, oh how I miss you..."

MYSTERIOUS SPATIAL RIFT

My friend Hachiro Tomoeda is a peculiar fellow. Sharing with you a few dreams he's told me about is the quickest way to give you a sense of just how peculiar he is.

Hachiro loves talking about his dreams. These tend to be extremely odd and surprisingly detailed, but as someone who rarely dreams myself, I found them intriguing and, at times, even disturbing.

"In my dreams, I visit the same city, again and again," he said, vacant eyes glaring at me.

"...So I get this feeling that *I've been to this city before*. Before I know it, all these people I've met in dreams are coming out of the woodwork: old men, young women, you name it. I talk to this strange group of people about what happened before, hoping to continue the long series of events from previous dreams. But, more often than not, the same thing happens in every dream, and whenever I get the feeling something is going to happen, it generally turns out that way. It sounds crazy, but my hunches often turn out to be right. However, there's another odd thing about these dreams: my face. In these dreams I always have the same face, and it's completely different from what you see now. My face isn't pale like this, it's more of a reddish copper color. Even its shape is completely different: longer, with a well-defined nose, larger mouth, and eyes aglow with a passion you'd never believe, not to mention a wonderful head of hair and a stately beard. That imposing man in my dreams is *me*. What do you think? Pretty strange, right? That's why I often have these strange thoughts. *Could this city, and these people in my dreams, actually exist? Could I possess two bodies with different faces, sharing a single soul?* Stuff like that. Oh, I can see you're having trouble believing me. It's written all over your face. Alright then, I'll tell you an even stranger, more disturbing story—one that will wipe that smile right off your face. It's a true story of something that just happened to me."

Chapter 1

One day, I had this dream.

I was walking down a long hallway. Oddly enough, there wasn't a single window. Everything was a yellow color—the walls, the ceiling—and at regular intervals on both sides of the extremely long hallway was a set of identical doors. I stood there, motionless except for my eyes inspecting each of the doorknobs, one by one. They all shared a dull brass color except for a shiny gold one on the fifth or sixth door down, on the left side if I remember correctly.

"A golden doorknob!"

When I came to the door with the shiny doorknob, my hand spontaneously reached out for it. Grabbing the golden doorknob, it twisted and pushed inward. Needless to say, the door opened easily each time I had this dream. I entered the room as if sucked in by some invisible force.

Inside was a bare living room, measuring roughly thirty square meters. A bright red carpet dominated the center, laid under a light blue table and set of chairs. On the table rested a green, Spanish-style flower vase that always contained a pink carnation.

The room had a very unusual design. I took quite a liking to it, especially the large mirror hanging on a far wall. The full-sized mirror stretched from floor to ceiling, larger than the kind you find in barbershops. It was over three meters wide, framed on both sides by a narrow curtain made from an ornate, heavy-looking fabric that hung down from a rod at the top. Unfortunately, the room's dim lighting obscured the curtain's color, although it appeared to be a dark shade of indigo. The mirror faithfully reflected the contents of the room, just as you would expect. Whenever I entered that room I was always eager to walk straight up to the mirror and see my reflection. Because the mirror was at the far end of the room, angled away from me, I had to be directly in front of it to see myself. I had a habit of staring into that mirror, fascinated by my stately visage. Thrusting my chest out, I would imagine this is what Victor Emmanuel the First must have looked like. My image in the mirror followed suit, his chest raised triumphantly.

But just as I was enjoying myself making funny faces and idiotic gestures into the mirror, a voice suddenly called out from behind.

"Would you like something to drink, sir...?"

It was the voice of a young man.

I turned around to discover a silver tray on the table with a liquor bottle and a drinking glass upon it. A handsome, athletic teenage boy—who had presumably just spoken—stood with his back to the door. But there was someone else: a young woman standing dangerously close to him. How did these two get here so quickly?

The woman, her eyes downcast at first, gradually raised her head and glared at me.

(What the...)

I suddenly averted my gaze as if struck by some great force, for the woman had been a lover of mine. Watching her waltz into the room with a young guy in tow, I was anything but calm.

However, getting hysterical now would only embarrass me. Maintaining perfect composure, I approached the table and sat down, facing away from the couple. I filled the glass with alcohol and silently raised it to my lips.

Behind me, I heard the frantic whispering of those two engaged in a private conversation. Their faint voices, intensified if as by an amplifier, thundered in my ears like a metal washbasin being pounded next to my head.

(Those two are far more than friends. I'm sure they've gone all the way!)

I struggled to hold back my emotions, but nothing could stop the rising anger. I shut my eyes, grabbed the glass, and gulped down the whole thing, then slammed it down on the table. The whispering died instantly.

I stayed calm and maintained my composure. Did those two come here just to show off? Did they really think I wouldn't notice? If so, fine with me. I know—I'll return the favor and pretend they don't exist.

Legs trembling, I planted my feet firmly on the floor and stood up from the chair. I walked quietly to the large mirror at the far end of the room, making sure to avoid looking in their direction.

Before I knew it, I was standing before the mirror. I watched the couple's reflection, their bodies all over each other, practically making love. The girl was taking the lead, trying to seduce him, but I detected a hint of hesitation in the boy. Blood rushed up from my legs into my head.

I looked at my face in the mirror and discovered my expression had completely changed. I saw my shoulders shaking uncontrollably. Oblivious to me observing them through the mirror, this indecent couple was in the middle of committing a depraved act. Panic began to creep in. I tried to scream, but nothing came out of my dry throat. I had to calm down...

I thought to enlist the aid of tobacco and pulled my cigarette case from my pocket. I tried to gently open the lid, keeping it hidden in the shadows of my body to avoid being seen, but for some reason it wouldn't open. Realizing I should be careful about what my face revealed, I shifted my eyes to look at the reflection of my hand in the mirror. Then I looked at the cigarette case.

(Huh?)

I was a little startled; the thing in my hand was not a cigarette case but a...

(...a pistol!)

My hand gripped none other than a small, boxy Browning pistol. A wave of vertigo washed over me.

That's when it happened. The reflection of my hand, still holding the pistol, quietly floated up to the level of my chest. Defying logic, the hand crept upwards against my own will. Equally strange was seeing my hand's reflection inch up slightly higher than my actual hand. It was incredibly disturbing to see the hand in the mirror somehow moving ahead of my own hand. I couldn't bear to stand here and do nothing; if I stayed still like this in front of the mirror, I would surely go insane. After all, the movement of my reflection, even as I stood frozen before the mirror, would be certain evidence that I could no longer be counted among the living.

(...)

A tremor ripped through my body, nearly tearing it apart. I quickly raised the arm holding the pistol, chasing after its reflection, and it soon caught up with the image in the mirror.

(My, that was horrific!)

My body was completely drenched with sweat.

The pistol had risen a good ways above my chest, where its muzzle pressed firmly into my left shoulder. I twisted my shoulder back gradually. I squinted and aimed the gun. Once my target was fixed, I continued to rotate my body back, ever so deliberately.

My attempt to speak only resulted in a pathetic stutter. The couple continued their flirting, completely unaware of what I was about to do.

"Y-you bitch!"

Detestable slut!

I glanced at the mirror to see a few teeth exposed as I bit down hard on my lower lip. Time slowed to a crawl, my tormented expression urging me to the only natural conclusion: my two fingers on the trigger retracted...

Bang.

Oh shit, I really did it.

"...Ugggghhhhh..."

The girl bent over backward as if struck by a bolt of electricity. One hand clutched her chest while the other flailed wildly in the air; a moment later, she collapsed there on the spot.

"I killed someone. After everything, I've committed murder with my own hands!"

I approached the girl sprawled on the floor, so still I would have sworn she was in a deep sleep. Her clothes had a gaping red hole near the chest where fresh blood gushed out, trickling over her partially exposed breasts and down her neck. The boy was nowhere to be found; I assumed he had darted out the room without me noticing.

"Shit, I just killed someone..." I mumbled.

Just then, I heard a derisive laugh in an all-too-familiar voice: my own.

"Oh...I get it. I'm having a dream where I murder someone...But if I'm not careful I'll wake up in the middle of the best part. My hands should be trembling more, like I've actually killed someone. And I should be scared. *Very* scared..."

Unfortunately, something happened and I lost my memory of everything after that. I only remember up to the point where I shot and killed the girl.

Chapter 2

I must have bored you to tears with so much detail, especially considering I was only talking about a dream. But I wanted you to understand just how vivid and strange my dreams are.

My talk about dreams isn't over yet. Now I'd like to tell you about an even more mysterious dream. I really hope you'll listen to what I have to say.

Let's see...I don't remember how many days had passed, but eventually I had another dream.

Just as I was making my way down a long hallway, I realized something.

"Another long hallway. The walls and ceiling are yellow, and..."

"I remember! I've been in this hallway before!" I thought to myself. But that quickly led to another, less desirable, realization.

"...Oh, I'm dreaming now. I'm really dreaming!"

As I walked down the hall, I tried to imitate my gait from the other day because I felt that otherwise I'd ruin a potentially wonderful dream...

Just like last time, I glanced at the doors one by one. I noticed a golden doorknob on the left side, five doors down.

"This is it," I said with a smile.

I turned the golden doorknob and slipped into the room. Needless to say, things looked exactly the same as before: a red carpet in the center, above that an elegant table and chair set in blue, and on the table, a green vase holding an identical pink carnation.

I chuckled under my breath as I made my way to the room's center, trying to keep from breaking out into laughter. From there, I inspected the far end of the room and found the large mirror. It was a great relief to see that mirror.

(I can imagine how in some occupations like acting, where each day the same movements are acted out with the same props, performances tend to get progressively easier after the first day—just like what I am experiencing now.)

Thoughts like this popped into my head.

The next moment, I found myself once again before the large mirror. The same stately appearance was reflected in it: a bold mustache surrounded by a storm of unkempt hair.

"Sir, would you like a..."

I looked behind me to see who had spoken and found the same handsome young man standing there. Beside him was the same young girl, eyes downcast, another character in this performance who hadn't changed at all.

Adhering to the proper order of events, I returned to the table. I opened the liquor bottle and filled up the glass. Right then, as if on cue, I heard the hushed whispers of that couple behind me.

Infuriated, I chugged the entire drink in a single breath. I slammed down the glass, sprung to my feet, and staggered towards the mirror...

An uncomfortable feeling came over me, triggered by the vivid recollection of that terrible incident the other day. The thing that happened next was utterly terrifying. No, I don't mean the part when I murdered someone; I mean when, standing before that large mirror, my reflection moved before I did. That uncanny sight, etched deeply in my mind...that was truly horrifying.

My body trembled uncontrollably. I carefully watched my every move reflected in the mirror, afraid of what I might see.

I withdrew from my pocket not a cigarette case, but a pistol...

Yes, now is my chance!

I raised the pistol to my chest ever so slowly...ever so deliberately...

"Well, well...it seems my reflection is following me well today."

I sighed, relieved to see no sign of the expected abnormality today. And yet, our movements could diverge at any moment...

"Whew, I'm safe..."

I was so happy, so relieved, that I nearly cried out. Nothing abnormal had occurred. I even tried flailing my arms up and down, but like a film with perfectly synchronized audio and video tracks, my reflection stayed in lockstep with its counterpart, moving the same way at the same time, without even the slightest gap.

(Perhaps that terrible *separation* I witnessed the other day was simply a hallucination?)

This thought came to me, but then I realized there was no need to think so deeply about it. After all, this was just a dream; there was no rule stating everything had to make sense. If, for example, I stood in the middle of a field and wished for a desk, it might appear out of nowhere, like magic. In dreams, things like that would be perfectly normal.

I held the gun tightly against my left shoulder, took aim, and slowly twisted my shoulder back. The girl and boy whispered to one another excitedly, panting as if out of breath. I heard the young girl's sensual moaning, you know the kind that can drive you crazy.

"Take this, asshole!"

I pulled the trigger.

Bang.

The girl's piercing shriek tore through the room.

Clutching her shoulder with one hand, she toppled over onto the carpet as her other arm twitched, clawing wildly at the air.

"Why is she still moving?"

I suspiciously approached the girl who was supposed to be dead from my gunshot. She was barely hanging on. But as I watched, her life faded away before my eyes. The bloodstained hand that had been clutching her shoulder gradually slid down, revealing a gaping wound that spurted fresh blood, a blooming flower. Her arms and legs twitched a few more times before collapsing to the floor, and her body finally went still.

"You put on quite a show in those final moments!"

Sneering, I approached her body and gave it a kick. It didn't budge, as if she was in a deep sleep. I circled around to her head and gazed at her face from the side.

"Huh?"

I had been certain this woman was my old girlfriend, but I was shocked when I saw her face.

"It's...not her."

The realization struck me like a massive weight. I cradled her limp head and angled her face towards me.

"Oh no, this is..."

I've made a terrible mistake. I was so sure it was my old girlfriend, but I couldn't have been more wrong; the woman's corpse before me was unmistakably the wife of a close friend who was like a brother to me.

"D-damn it!"

My teeth clenched. Why hadn't I realized this sooner? Clearly, murder was a terrible crime, but to shoot dead the wife of a good friend...how could I ever make it up to him?

She had been a truly admirable woman. Her husband was a good friend of mine, but strange rumors about him had been circulating lately. Apparently he was making a great profit by loaning out money at an exorbitant interest rate but rarely returned home to see his wife waiting there alone. She would often visit me, worried sick, prostrating herself teary-eyed and begging that I help repair her relationship with her husband, seemingly gone sour due to her inadequacies. I had never met a nicer, more good-natured woman in my life, and I failed to understand how any man could pretend to know nothing of this woman and neglect his duties as a husband.

Thus, I began to pity this woman, consoling her whenever the opportunity arose. After visiting me she would always return home in a better mood. However, it seems that lately my friend had an odd suspicion of something going on between his wife and me. He was worried about us being alone frequently together in the same room, a concern I found both idiotic and maddening. How truly unfortunate.

"And now I have murdered that woman with my own hands. What am I going to do..."

I was too ashamed to face my friend, but I was even more remorseful toward his wife, whom I had shot dead. But at the same time, I would no longer be able to prove my innocence of the alleged relationship between us. I lay down beside her body, tormented by an excruciating pain like my intestines were being ripped apart...

"...How could have I been such a fool? I'm crying in the middle of a dream!"

I suddenly heard the sound of my own voice. Oh, it's all just a dream.

The entrance burst open and a crowd clamored into the room. At its head stood the attractive young man I had seen with my friend's wife, but when he saw me, he backed away and disappeared into the crowd.

"You're under arrest!"

A group of people wearing police officer uniforms rushed at me and restrained my arms. Just as I was thinking about how I would be executed soon, handcuffs were slapped on my wrists. I have no memory of what happened after that.

Well now, what do you think of these two dreams? Pretty strange, huh? Aren't they almost *too* vivid?

Chapter 3

It was a quiet winter morning.

A high fence obscured the sun, but the sky was clear for miles, a refreshing scent of citrus in the air.

Enclosed by the plain, white walls of the square room, my friend Hachiro Tomoeda was telling me once again about his dreams.

Sometimes my mind gets all messed up and causes me a great deal of trouble. I know it's not because of my age, but my life is often thrown into disarray by my tendency to mix things up.

I think I was telling you the other day about two similar dreams where I killed someone, but I don't remember how far I got. Most likely I stopped around the part where I was thrown in jail, awaiting a trial. Yeah, that sounds about right.

I remember talking about those dreams in earnest, unaware of my absurd misconception, but perhaps things didn't happen like that. To be honest, during that conversation I was convinced you were not a person from a dream, but from the real world. However, after being implicated in a murder and then talking to you in this jail cell, it's clear that you're also from the dream world. Why did it take me so long to realize this?

This is not easy for me since I'm hopelessly poor at explanations. But if you don't mind, I'll try once more. I told you about that murder incident; after that, I was jailed as a suspect. Sometimes you would come to visit me in jail, proof that the world where the murder occurred and the world you live in is one and the same. I spoke to you about the murder in my dream. Also, if you ask me, you yourself are from the same dream world. The way I see it, that murder took place in my dreams; to you, it took place in the world that you live in. But, you see, *this* is the dream world now where I am speaking...When a dimwit like me tries thinking about this stuff, I always get totally confused. Maybe I should just let someone else figure it all out. Anyway, I'll tell you what happened next.

Like I said, at some point I discovered *myself*, jailed and awaiting trial. I was astonished to learn it was related to a murder in that room with the big mirror.

"My, what a terribly long dream I'm having..."

I didn't find this out until later, but at the time I was apparently about to be put into a mental institution. So I'm really glad I figured everything out when I did.

After that they investigated me at length, and one of the court officials was a kind-hearted magistrate by the name of Sugiura. One day he came to me and started telling me a story. It was a mysterious tale skillfully crafted by a true creative genius, filled with uncanny events like you often find in short stories. While clearly a fabrication, I was intrigued to see how everything was woven together, so I'd like to tell you about it.

"Do you think those two dreams were really dreams? Even assuming they are, don't you see an inconsistency between them?" the judge suddenly asked me, his tone reserved.

I kept quiet; these questions irritated me. He continued babbling, even more sure of himself. This is what he told me:

"You said you killed an old girlfriend in your first dream, and a friend's wife in the second. If, as you say, you are seeing the same events repeatedly in dreams, then shouldn't the victim be the same each time? Don't you think it's odd that the person you murdered was different?"

"Anything is possible in dreams," I objected. "Characters can switch around arbitrarily."

The man's questions continued.

"In your first dream, when you killed your girlfriend, there was a simplicity, a surreal beauty. And yet, your second dream—where you killed your friend's wife—wasn't it painted in colors that seemed almost too vivid? Didn't you detect something *deliberate* about this disparity?" he said, a deadly serious expression on his face.

The moment I heard this, I thought he really was on to something. The murder in the second dream did have a much deeper sense of realism. However, once I thought about it a little more, I realized he was badly distorting minor details just to argue his point, and this disgusted me.

"You're quiet, but I think you understand what I'm saying, at least a little," Judge Sugiura added, delivering another one-sided statement.

"Listen, I'll tell you a few more discrepancies. First, what do you think of that room? What a truly unusual place. When you walk in, you're greeted by a large mirror covering the wall, like in a barbershop, and an oddly remarkable red carpet. Even the plain colors of the table and chair set, their placement, and the flower on display were unusual. If someone was actually living there, you would expect a clutter of items; but those were nowhere to be found, and the room's remarkable simplicity made it hard to forget once you saw it. Like the handiwork of a magician, it had the appearance of a room, yet was totally unfit for human habitation. Nothing more than a prop in a trick."

"Come on, dreams are supposed to be remarkable and simple," I wanted to say, but I kept quiet.

"So what do you think? I bet all of this is starting to make sense to you," the magistrate said, increasingly confident.

"Now there's one final, truly great contradiction. I'm sure you remember the terrifying part of your first dream. That's where the contradiction was. You grabbed the pistol and saw it in your reflection in the mirror. Then, strangely enough, you watched your hand raise above your chest, stopping somewhere near your left shoulder. Yet your actual hand hovered there unmoving, gripping the pistol you'd withdrawn from your pocket. In short, you had observed a gap between your actual body's movements and your reflection in the mirror, a sight which terrified you to no end. By witnessing a mysterious rift between the spatial region encompassing your body, presumably possessing a single soul, and that of your body's reflection, you were thrown into complete and needless confusion. Had you been an ordinary person with a sound mind, you would have surely realized the truth. This point is critically important. What would an ordinary person think? *How strange...I'm not in a haunted house, but the reflection in this mirror before me is moving separately from my body. This can't be right. The image in the mirror isn't my reflection!* Just like that, you should have figured it out. In other words, the large mirror before you was not actually a mirror; behind that panel of glass stood a person disguised as you, trying to make you believe he was your reflection. You should have picked up on that immediately. If you were an ordinary person, that is."

This was a shock to even someone as dull as me, as if a hammer had suddenly struck my skull. But shock soon became anger as I began to question whether such an absurd thing was even possible.

"After all, the entire room's interior was reflected in that mirror: the chairs, the table, and the bottle of liquor. But that's not all. Even the girl and her handsome companion were reflected in the mirror. Is something that absurd actually possible?" I objected.

"It's like I've been telling you. That room was specially prepared for the deception. What you thought was a reflection in the mirror was, in actuality, a separate room visible through a large pane of glass, made to appear identical to the room you were in. They just needed to put everything in the same location, turned to face the pane of glass. Same thing with the people. There were two different couples, one in each room, so each person appeared to have a reflection. In fact, there was another man in the far room. As I said, he was dressed just like you. In any case, not in your right mind, you mistook the faces of the two couples to be identical. After that point, it would have been easy to deceive anyone, even an ordinary person. Well now, let's consider why someone would create dual rooms and make them appear to represent a single space. That couldn't be any more obvious. The man disguised as you suggested your next action: aiming the pistol and shooting the girl behind you. The gunshot sound was probably from a blank cartridge and, as planned, she collapsed on the spot. Finally, in dramatic fashion she triggered the release of red iron oxide concealed in something like an eggshell, giving the impression of having been shot dead."

"If that's true, then why would he make me do such a thing?" I cried out.

"That's obvious. They planned to lure you to the place of your second dream and have you actually murder your friend's wife. They fooled you, a weak-minded man, into believing you were reliving the same dream, making you fire the pistol again in the second dream, just like the first. But the second time, the pistol was loaded with live ammunition and the second room was not used. By darkening that room, the pane of glass functioned like a mirror. It's a trick commonly employed in circus attractions; everyone knows about it. But in any case you have, unintentionally, murdered a woman."

"But why me?" I shouted back at the judge.

"I investigated and found out the reason. It was the woman's own husband who plotted to kill her—in other words, your friend. He was the one who orchestrated it all."

"No, my friend would never do something so horrible," I said.

"There's no use defending him. We've already gathered sufficient evidence. Your friend is quite a despicable fellow. His failed business venture demanded a great deal of money, and there was a life insurance policy on his wife for an enormous sum. He couldn't just kill his wife with his own hands, so he tried to use you instead. Apparently he even fabricated an excuse to lure his wife to that room. She was brought inside and saw you who had, according to the rumors, gone insane. Then you shot and killed her. In any case, I'm glad your mental state has recovered so quickly since arriving here."

As I listened, I was nearly fooled by his well-crafted story. Could my friend really have plotted such an elaborate scheme? I felt there was something wrong with the judge's logic.

"But Mr. Magistrate, something doesn't seem right. How did my friend manage to manipulate me so easily?"

"Isn't that obvious too? Did you not have the habit of explaining your dreams to him in great detail? He used that to take advantage of you."

So you see, my friend, that's what I was told. I really pity the magistrate for wasting so much time fretting over these minute details, because he's claiming that you used me to kill your own wife to avoid dirtying your own hands. I can't believe he has the audacity to say those things about you. Fortunately, everything happened in a dream so it doesn't really matter. Had it actually happened, we would be in some serious trouble.

But, you see, that magistrate just wouldn't give up. What a pain in the ass.

"You're mistaken about those things happening in a dream. If you still believe that, then I'll just have to prove to you how wrong you are..." the magistrate said.

When I asked him what he had in mind, he led me to a mirror.

"So which is it?" he asked. "Is the face you see reflected here the one from your dreams, or the one from the real world?"

When I looked in the mirror, a sickly pale, very round face stared back at me. It was nothing like the stately visage I'd seen in my dreams.

"It's my face from the real world," I answered honestly.

With that, the magistrate continued, an unspoken *I told you* in his eyes.

"Now isn't that strange. You've been saying this is all a dream. But if the face you saw now was your real face, that's really strange. Am I wrong? Now listen up. You've got to think hard and remember everything. This dream world that you believe in has never existed. There's only one reality. You claimed there was an alternate reality where you had a different face, but in the end your two faces are one and the same. Are you following me? When your mental condition deteriorates, you become like a completely different person. You stop combing your hair, let your beard grow out. There are even times where you've run around half-naked outside, eventually hiding somewhere in the mountains. You get a sunburn there and your appearance drastically changes. Let's try one more thing while I have you here. First, ruffle your well-combed hair and make it stand up all over. Next, put on this fake beard I have here. Then we'll apply some brown facial powder...Now take a look at your face in the mirror. Does it ring a bell? I bet it's exactly like the face you thought you had in the other reality," he said with a chuckle.

I was utterly shocked. The magistrate was right...But wait a minute, something was still fishy. His skill in solving this case appeared impeccable, yet the truth was far from that. He knew practically nothing about math, and his logic was completely off. In other words, he had secretly retouched my face in the dream world with makeup to make it look identical to my real face. Then he had undone that disguise to return my dream face to its prior state. This by no means proves the magistrate's one-sided story. I knew it, I'm definitely dreaming.

That sure was a close call. It's like I've been saying, my friend: we're both in the middle of a dream now...

Just then, the steel door opened with a creak. As I expected, the head prison guard silently entered carrying handcuffs, followed by the warden, skinny as a bird, and the prison chaplain who resembled a large potato wrapped in a gold brocade vestment.

"If you'll pardon me for interrupting you..." said the prison guard. "The time has come to execute the prisoner's sentence, so Mr. Tomoeda, I'd like to ask you to leave."

My friend stood up abruptly from his chair. He embraced me, glaring at the others.

"You mustn't be afraid. Whatever anyone says, this is all part of a dream, even if you are about to climb the gallows. You mustn't believe you're actually going to die, because ultimately, you're just dreaming about being executed. There's absolutely nothing to be afraid of...As soon as you get too uncomfortable, just wake up from this dream. I'm sure a moment later you'll find yourself in a warm bed, hearing your children in the next room switching on the radio to listen to the morning calisthenics. Don't stay there mulling about the terrible dream you just had; quickly jump out of bed so you aren't late to work. Well then, if you'll excuse me..." And with that, he left my prison cell.

Yes, yes! I knew it was a dream! Gallows...bring on the gallows!

THE LIVING INTESTINE

Peculiar Medical Student

Once again, from early in the morning medical student Ryuji Fukiya couldn't stop thinking about the intestine.

When the clock struck 3 p.m., he went out.

The place he called home was a strange makeshift hut situated below the arch of an elevated railway.

Now this fellow Ryuji, who lived in such a very strange place, was himself a very strange medical student; even though he was not an assistant, he had already attended medical college for seven years—the only genuinely long-term medical student in Japan.

This situation occurred because he had made it a point to not be greedy and only take the elective exams for his favorite subjects. That's why he had five subject exams left to take even though seven years had passed since his admission.

He rarely went to the campus, spending most of his life quietly in that strange house in the midst of the city's clamor.

No more than two people had ever stepped foot in that house. One was the landlord, the other a person he was planning on calling now about the intestine, Professor Kumamoto.

He approached a public phone in front of the train station, pale face framed by long tasseled hair resembling that of a lion and emaciated body covered by a black school uniform sporting shiny, well-worn metal buttons.

His call was directed at the hospital associated with a certain prison holding 2,700 prisoners. Because female nurses were not permitted there, the hospital had only male nurses. It was common knowledge that male prisoners shouldn't be allowed to see women.

"Hello, this is the prison hospital."

"Right, the prison hospital...Yeah, I want to talk to Professor Kumamoto. Who am I? Tell him it's Inomata." For some reason he used a fake name, his overt arrogance frightening the telephone operator across the copper wire.

"Hey Kumamoto. I'm sure you know why I'm calling. It's going to be ready today, right? You're certain? I assume you've actually prepared the intestine for me...OK, third window from the south. You see, I've been thinking about what to do if this doesn't work out. I'll probably have you lose your job and then go starving...Oh no, I'm not threatening you. Just follow my instructions without complaining and you'll be fine...I'll be there, definitely. Eleven at night."

He ended the call, a distasteful conversation no one would enjoy having.

Professor Kumamoto was the head of surgery at the prison's hospital, an amiable man praised by all. With kids, a lovely manikin wife, and no small amount of savings built up, he was considered the epitome of success.

However, for some reason Ryuji had a bad habit of verbally attacking the professor without even giving him a chance to defend himself. According to Ryuji, Professor Kumamoto was not just a despicable quack, he was a scheming intellectual who deserved the cruelest treatment.

Ryuji took full advantage of Professor Kumamoto even as he disparaged him, a man whose educational background far surpassed his own; he continually exploited the professor like a slave, all while enjoying a host of benefits from the relationship.

I assume you've prepared the intestine for me.

Judging from what Ryuji had just said on the phone, it appeared he was making a threat to Professor Kumamoto.

But what did "prepare the intestine" mean? And what was Ryuji plotting?

The answer to these questions would have to wait until 11 o'clock that night.

Third Window

It was already 10:58 p.m.

A medical student bumped into the prison hospital's small steel gate.

"This place sure closes early," he complained and tried to push it open.

The steel gate opened easily. It hadn't been locked; a heavy concrete block placed at its base had kept it closed.

"Hello..."

The guard bowed deeply in response to Ryuji's greeting. He didn't know why, but any medical student who spoke so informally to the eminent Dr. Kumamoto was, despite his uncultured appearance, most likely a blood relative of the professor's prior feudal lord. At least that was the guard's optimistic thinking. Therefore, at the gate he always gave this student the most formal of greetings.

With a derisive snort the ragged-clothed, lion-faced Ryuji walked past the guard, heading towards a group of shrubs inside the dim hospital.

He quickened his pace, easily weaving through the plants of the dark courtyard garden like an owl. Before long, the building of the fourth ward appeared before him.

(Third window from the south...)

He approached the window calmly. Below it lay a crate similar to those that hold mandarin oranges. This must be a gesture of kindness from the professor, Ryuji thought and mounted it like a stepping stool. He heaved open the heavy window.

The window slid up effortlessly. Without a doubt, its smooth movement was a result of the professor having greased the window's pulley in advance.

Finally, he was able to grab hold of the thick, meter-long glass tube from the table sitting right in front of his face.

"Well, well, look what we have here!"

Ryuji held the bulky glass tube up to the streetlight shining above the exterior wall. The tube was filled to the top with a clear liquid. Inside was something slimy, with an unusual color neither gray nor lavender.

"Yes...I've finally gotten my hands on what I've wanted for so long. What a truly marvelous specimen!"

Delighted, Ryuji lowered the window back in place. He held the stolen glass tube like a thick walking stick and climbed down to the ground.

"Ahh...there's nothing quite like a night garden walk."

Ryuji's greeting as he passed before the gate was nothing like his usual self. But there was no question whatsoever that he was tickled pink from tonight's loot.

"Oh, thank you very much, sir."

The guard, stiffening his body, appeared to be truly thankful for Ryuji's greeting.

After passing through the gate, Ryuji hurried away in his wooden clogs, the thick tube resting upon his shoulders. Three hours later, he finally arrived home. The city was dead silent as if passed out from exhaustion.

He managed to enter the house without being seen by anyone. Inside, he turned on a light.

"Yes...truly marvelous indeed. What a truly wonderful intestine!"

Ryuji held up the glass tube to the light and stared at it in awe.

The thing he had called the "intestine" sat stagnant within the blue-tinged liquid.

"Oh, it's alive!"

Upon closer inspection, the lavender-colored intestine wriggled back and forth in the Ringer's solution. *Splosh splosh.*

A living intestine!

A living intestine—the very thing Ryuji had badgered Professor Kumamoto persistently for the past year. The professor had complied with all of Ryuji's other requests; this was the only one that had taken such a long time.

"So what's the problem, professor? You have 2,900 male prisoners there. Some are facing capital punishment, and there must be others who get appendicitis or die from some unusual cause. There's no way you can't sneak out a measly 100-centimeter intestine for me. Hey asshole, if you don't do as I say, I guess I'll just have to do what we talked about. If you don't like that, you better listen up, and quickly."

Finally, after a full year of blackmailing the professor in this way, Ryuji had acquired the long-awaited living intestine.

But this begs the question of why Ryuji desired such a disgusting thing in the first place. Perhaps it was to fulfill his need to collect rare items.

Not quite.

Ringer's Solution Ecology

A living intestine. In the medical literature, this was not a particularly unusual thing.

If you look in a physiology textbook, you'd find a score of intestines—guinea pig, rabbit, dog, even human—all living in Ringer's solution.

Specimens of living intestines were not very difficult to find either.

But what Ryuji secretly took great pride in was the large, magnificent intestine before him, longer than a walking cane at 100 centimeters, squirming vigorously even now within the Ringer's solution. You aren't likely to find such a fine specimen anywhere on the planet. Ryuji bowed deeply towards the glass tube in great respect for the unmatched skill of Professor Kumamoto.

Ryuji made the living intestine the centerpiece of the room. He dangled a string from the ceiling and tied it to the end of the tube, below which he placed a stand to hold the tube.

The medical student's room was already a strange sight: a space crammed with piles of musty medical textbooks, rusty unidentifiable surgical tools, and various other medical devices. But with the addition of this rare guest, the room's odd atmosphere was finally complete.

Ryuji placed a tall, three-legged stool in front of the glass tube that hung from the ceiling. He sat on the stool and stared at the strange human organ squirming within the clear liquid, his arms crossed as if mesmerized by the sight.

Splosh splosh splosh.

Splut splut splut.

As he watched, the intestine's entire body twisted this way and that in a complex series of expressions beyond anything the human face was capable of.

"How odd. As I watch this little fellow, I feel that it's a life form far more advanced than humans."

With these words he had, albeit unintentionally, made an astute observation that transcended logic.

After that Ryuji, body stiff as a statue before the glass tube, gazed unblinking at the living intestine for long stretches of time, almost as if he himself would become the intestine.

He reduced his meals and, though unpleasant to say, his bowel movements to the absolute minimum. He dreaded stepping away from the living intestine for even a minute or two.

This continued for three days straight.

Finally, having fallen asleep on the stool from several exhausting days of constant tension, his own raucous snoring snapped him awake. The room was pitch black.

Ryuji had a bad feeling. He jumped off the stool and flipped on the light switch. He was concerned that someone had stolen his precious living intestine.

"Ahh, what a relief."

The glass tube holding the intestine was still there, hanging from the ceiling.

But the next moment Ryuji cried out in a voice approaching a shriek.

"Oh no, this is terrible. It's not moving!"

Ryuji fell back onto his bottom with a thud. He tore frantically at his hair like a madman, lost in a dark maelstrom of desperation.

"W–wait a second..."

Face flushed red, he stood up. He grabbed a burette and climbed up onto the stool.

He filled up the burette with clear liquid from the glass tube, then dumped it into the drain.

He took down a bottle labeled "1/10000 choline" from the drug shelf and inserted an empty burette into it.

The liquid rose up into the burette.

Ryuji jumped nimbly back onto the stool. He carefully transferred the choline from the burette to the glass tube.

The liquid disappeared into the Ringer's solution without a sound.

Ryuji's eyes were truly something to behold as he stared intensely at the contents of the tube. But a moment later, a smile emerged on his face.

"It's moving!"

The intestine began to squirm again. *Slosh slosh slosh.*

"I can't believe I forgot the choline! There must be something wrong with me."

He sighed deeply in embarrassment, almost like a little girl.

"The intestine still lives. But I must start the conditioning at once, otherwise it may not survive much longer."

He rolled up his shirt sleeves and put his arms into the stained surgical gown hanging on the wall.

The Amazing Experiment

Ryuji was brimming with life, as if he were a completely different person.

"Alright, it's conditioning time!"

But what exactly was Ryuji going to condition? He gathered various items while circling the room: hoses, purifiers, stands.

"Yes...I will triumph in this epoch-making experiment and show the world..."

He mumbled to himself while gathering retorts, wire netting, and Bunsen burners.

Standing in the middle of the large pile of equipment he'd gathered, like a stage carpenter Ryuji began assembling the equipment for his experiment.

In a short span of time the structure of glass, metal, and liquids grew to a massive scale. It appeared to be centered around the living intestine.

A switch was flipped and the power light went from blue to red. In the corner of the room, a pump motor began spinning with a low rumble.

An eerie gleam intensified in Ryuji's eyes as he worked.

What was he trying to do?

Electric current began to flow as a light blue flame rose from the Bunsen burner.

Two smaller glass tubes were inserted into the larger tube containing the living intestine.

From one, tiny bubbles emerged.

Nibbling on a pencil, Ryuji Fukiya hung a large board from his neck on a string and used colored pencils to mark up the graph paper it held as he alternated between a current meter, thermometer, and hydrometer.

A group of curves gradually trended upwards on the paper: red, blue, purple, black.

In the process, he frequently passed before the glass tube and cocked his head to the side, scrutinizing the ever-squirming intestine.

He continued the grueling experiment, literally going without food or sleep; it was truly a superhuman effort.

When he compared the intestine's condition between 6 o'clock in the morning and nine at night, he discovered a tiny, yet noticeable change.

Then, twelve hours later, he observed another change.

As the experiment progressed, the temperature of the Ringer's solution gradually rose to a point, after which its density progressively decreased.

On the fourth day of the experiment, the liquid inside the glass tube had become mostly water.

On the sixth day, the liquid was no longer visible; in its place, a cloud of pinkish gas swirled.

The intestine in the tube continued its incessant twitching, seemingly unaware of the disappearance of the liquid.

A stiff smile reminiscent of a festival mask was plastered on Ryuji's face.

"Yes, yes...I've already written a new page in the medical history books with my achievement. An intestine living within a gas! What an amazing experiment!"

He connected a bunch of new devices in succession, then removed the old ones.

By the eighth day, the gas inside of the glass tube had turned completely colorless and transparent.

By the ninth day, the Bunsen burner went out. The bubbling gas stopped.

By the tenth day, even the sound of the motor ceased. A thick silence fell over the laboratory like long-abandoned ruins.

That was right around 3 a.m.

For the next twenty-four hours he left the intestine completely alone, being careful not to disturb it.

It was the next day at 3 a.m., twenty-four hours later. He cautiously brought his face up close to the tube.

The intestine within the glass tube wriggled around lively as ever—but now in an environment of room temperature and normal humidity. *Splosh splosh.*

Ryuji Fukiya had, through a special procedure of his own design, succeeded in an experiment never before attempted by any other medical student in history: the survival of an intestine in breathable air.

Cohabitation

Ryuji learned how to play with the living intestine, now lying stretched out on the table before him.

The living intestine had, in a surprising development, begun to respond as if it possessed emotions.

When he used a syringe to insert a small amount of sugar water into one of the intestine's orifices, the organ began to squirm around vigorously. A moment later, a segment of the intestine extended out from the table towards him, as if begging for more sugar water.

"Alright, I get it. You want more sugar water. I'll give it to you. But only a little."

Ryuji offered another small drop of sugar water to the living intestine.

(What a sophisticated creature!)

He was speechless with awe.

Sometimes, playing with the living intestine that he had himself conditioned felt like a dream.

For some time now, Ryuji had entertained an outrageous theory.

If an intestine can survive with a portion of itself immersed in Ringer's solution, then it should be able to survive outside of that solution, so long as it is placed in an appropriate nutritional environment.

In other words, the same conditions for survival provided to the intestine by Ringer's solution could be provided via some equivalent nutritional environment.

At this juncture, he hypothesized that if a human intestine was truly a living thing, it would probably have nerves and might even adapt itself in response to its environment. So as long as he could provide adequate nutrition to the living intestine, it should be possible to condition it to survive in an environment of breathable air—or so went his theory.

Beginning with that premise, he did comprehensive research on such a possibility. As a result of that, about a year ago he finally gained some measure of confidence in his theory.

At last, his experiment was a great success. And to top it off, the experiment took surprisingly little effort.

A certain researcher once said that success was determined not by contemplating something, but by actually attempting it yourself. And he couldn't have been more right.

But when Ryuji thought about how a *living intestine*—a conception of his that, on the surface, seemed absurd—was squirming on the table before his very eyes, it all seemed so unreal.

It should also be noted that the intestine he had coaxed to survive in breathable air had begun to exhibit various intriguing, and unexpected responses.

One example of this was, as just explained, how the intestine had expressed a desire for more sugar water.

But that wasn't all. While playing with the intestine, Ryuji had discovered it had a surprisingly diverse set of reactions.

When he prodded the living intestine with the end of a thin platinum probe and passed a 600 MHz oscillating current through it, the intestine suddenly spewed forth a slimy mucus.

Later, in an experiment where he used tuning forks to apply sounds of certain specific frequencies to one region of the living intestine's body, he quickly discovered that this region was extremely sensitive to sound; it appeared to have developed an ability like the human eardrum. From this, he believed that the living intestine could probably even hear him speak.

Now that the intestine was exposed to the air, its surface began to slowly dry out. Something akin to an epidermal layer peeled off repeatedly. Eventually the living intestine became covered in a skin strongly resembling pale human lips.

On the 15th day after the living intestine was born, measured from the day it learned to survive in open air, the new organism developed to the point where it could freely crawl around Ryuji's room, whether upon a table or a book.

"Hey, Chiko. I left some sugar water for you here."

"Chiko" was the nickname he gave to the living intestine.

Ryuji called out while clapping his hands next to a shallow dish filled with sugar water, whereupon Chiko gleefully raised its back (if intestines even can be said to have backs) tall like a mountain. Once Chiko got hungry, the creature inched along the ground towards the dish and then sipped at the sugar water, producing little splashing sounds. It was a truly terrifying sight.

Once his experiment to raise Chiko the living intestine had reached a good stopping point, Ryuji thought it was almost time to write his groundbreaking research paper and shock the medical scientists of the world.

Then one day, exactly 120 days after Chiko had been 'born,' Ryuji decided he would finally begin drafting his research paper on the following day. But first, he wanted to get out of the house for a little while.

In the blink of an eye autumn had come and nearly gone, and outside the dry leaves of the Oriental plane tree rustled along the pavement, blown by the wind. The temperature was slowly dropping. Had Ryuji been living alone, things might have been different, but he had to spend this winter together with Chiko. So he thought he would go to the city to pick up a few things like a working electric stove.

The cans he had stocked up on were all gone and he wanted to replace those as well. He was hoping to make various types of soup for Chiko.

In over a hundred days, he hadn't left the house even once.

"I'm going out for a little while. There's a big portion of sugar water I made for you on the table in the corner."

With a sudden yearning for the outside world, he hurriedly told Chiko about the food, unlocked his front door, and dashed out onto the street.

Miscalculation

Ryuji Fukiya enjoyed himself to his heart's content for a full seven days before returning home.

The instant he stepped outside he found a world of wonderful comfort and joy waiting there for him. A flood of instincts surged through his spine as if a dam had broken. Driven by these he stayed up all night, day after day, enjoying himself as he caroused through the pleasure district. On the seventh day, his senses finally returned to him.

He had become a little concerned about Chiko's food. The sugar water should have been nearly empty after this many days.

"Well, I guess one more day won't hurt," he reconsidered and continued his spree.

That night, for some reason he began heading towards that prison hospital. There he paid a visit to Professor Kumamoto.

The professor was shocked when he saw Ryuji sitting in the waiting room, for there was now something undeniably primitive about the student.

"How did that thing a few months ago turn out?" the professor asked in a soft voice.

"Oh, you mean the living intestine? I'll be publishing my findings on that in due time," he chuckled.

"How many days did it survive?"

"I'll publish that eventually," he chuckled. "But Kumamoto, I discovered an intestine can actually express emotions. It's almost like...it was able to express something like human affection. I'm serious. This was a great surprise. Sometimes it even seemed like—oh, by the way, which prisoner's intestine was it? Tell me his name."

The professor didn't answer.

Normally, when the professor ignored him like this Ryuji would give him a thorough scolding. But today, apparently in extremely good spirits, he just smiled while stroking his chin.

"One more thing, Kumamoto. Can you gather all the available literature on hormones for me? Speaking of hormones, what happened to that cute telephone operator who worked at the hospital? You know, that 24-year-old single girl who was such a hard worker," Ryuji said with a lewd grin as he stared at the professor's face.

"Oh, you mean *that* girl..." the professor said, his face suddenly pale.

"That girl died of appendicitis. It was q-quite a while ago."

"She died, huh? Well, then I guess it's too late."

Ryuji sounded like he had lost all interest in the girl in an instant. He told the professor he'd come back later and hurried out of the room.

It was now 1 o'clock in the middle of the night.

On the eighth day, Ryuji finally returned home.

He inserted the key awkwardly into the front door.

(Maybe I overdid things a bit. That living intestine, I had given it the nickname "Chiko," right? I wonder if Chiko is still alive. On second thought, I don't really care if it's dead anyway. I already have enough data to shock the world.)

He unlocked the front door.

He opened it and stepped inside.

The room reeked of mold. But somewhere in the air, Ryuji thought he detected a hint of feminine body odor.

(That's strange.)

The room was pitch black.

He felt along the wall for the switch and turned it on.

The light came on instantly.

Eyes squinting against the brightness, he looked around the room.

There was no sign of Chiko on the table, or anywhere else for that matter.

(Oh, I guess Chiko didn't survive. Or maybe that thing escaped out to the street through a crack.)

Just then, it occurred to him to look at the glass bowl where he had left sugar water before going out.

Half of the sugar water remained. He screamed out in surprise.

"What the...I was sure that the sugar water would have been completely gone by now. What did that thing do?"

The very instant he spoke those words, it happened.

Accompanied by a weird howling sound, something white and cane-shaped sprang towards him at blinding speed.

It wrapped itself around his neck before he even had a chance to be surprised.

"Ugh..."

A tremendous force constricted his neck. He flailed his arms briefly, then collapsed to the floor.

It was not until a half year later that Ryuji Fukiya's body was found. The landlord had come to collect the rent for the year. Only a skeleton remained.

No one ever learned of his cause of death.

Likewise, no one ever learned of his groundbreaking experiment: *Chiko the living intestine.*

Everything about the living intestine experiment disappeared from history.

However, once in a great while, Professor Kumamoto thought about the intestine that he'd given to Ryuji. Truth be told, it had not come from a prisoner.

Then whose abdomen had the intestine been removed from?

It had been taken from that 24-year-old virgin who worked as a telephone operator at the prison hospital. She had died from appendicitis. But once you know that Professor Kumamoto was the acting surgeon at the time, no further explanation should be necessary.

Even Professor Kumamoto, who had secretly rejoiced over Ryuji's death, never knew that the living intestine cut from that virgin's abdomen had strangled Ryuji.

Not to mention how Chiko, the living intestine, had grown a great affection for Ryuji during the 120 days they lived together, or how Chiko, overjoyed upon hearing the voice of Ryuji after his eight-day absence, had wrapped itself around his neck, regrettably strangling him to death—a bizarre turn of events that the professor surely could never have imagined.

But it was Ryuji—failing to realize the living intestine had come from, of all people, a woman like that—who had done a truly unfortunate thing.

THE LAST BROADCAST

"When will our planet be destroyed? According to astronomers' calculations, the end of this planet will be caused by a collision with another planet, scattering it to pieces that vanish like a cloud of smoke, an event not likely to occur for billions of years. But that is an outright lie; the time of our world's destruction is close at hand, only ten minutes from now! I say this in all seriousness..."

As he listened, Yukichi Amano unconsciously leaned in towards the receiver, squeezing his headphones tightly with both hands. Although possibly some sort of joke or trick, this was nevertheless an extraordinarily strange thing to hear.

It was especially strange considering he was now listening to the voice of a lifeform inhabiting a planet other than Earth; in fact, sometimes even the inventor Yukichi himself had doubts about whether the amazing ability of the *VHF diffraction-modulated receiver*, the culmination of all his hard work, was but a figment of his imagination.

Yet the inspiration for inventions (by no means limited to the VHF diffraction-modulated receiver) often comes from the most trivial of coincidences, which is why, in retrospect, even the greatest inventions fail to surprise. On the contrary, there isn't a single person who doesn't wonder why it took so long to think up such an obvious idea.

Yukichi Amano's invention was inspired by one such coincidence. With a mouth full of pressed mollusk sushi after having rushed to a certain *Hanamaruya* Osaka-style sushi restaurant in Ginza for an early lunch, he glanced at a row of fish cakes arrayed neatly inside a glass case when the idea for the invention came to him, as if lightning had struck a mirror and reflected back onto him. He instantly sprang up from his chair and thrust out both hands towards the glass case, frightening the waitress as he blurted out, "Yes, that's it! That's it!"

It was then that Yukichi made up his mind, flagging down a car driving by and ordering the driver, "To Shinjuku, on the double!" The Taxi howled as it sped down the road. Yukichi quickly closed the car's roof and worked out the details of his new idea for the next ten minutes, his gaze darting frantically around the car's interior until he gained a certain degree of confidence in the idea.

In the end, he constructed the VHF diffraction-modulated receiver based on two fundamental principles: how VHF signals with a wavelength of 16 meters are most likely to penetrate the conducting Heaviside layer surrounding the Earth, and how the emotions of living beings can be expressed with oscillatory waveforms. At first, things didn't go as expected, so he tried rebuilding various parts, eventually resulting in a mechanism 150 times more sensitive than the first attempt. After realizing how the device could easily pick up radio signals from distant planets thousands of light-years away, he hit upon the idea of modulating the transmission to the universal language of Esperanto so it could be understood.

When Yukichi set up the latest version of the receiver in his attic, he was plagued by a terrible apprehension about becoming the first person on Earth to hear the spoken language of a lifeform from another planet. He wondered what mysterious civilization had developed there and what strange ideas they might try to express. A peculiar sort of excitement overcame him, as if fumbling around blind in a dark room filled with treasure; it was almost like a thin paper curtain separated him and some presence whose existence was undeniable. *That* was how deeply he believed in the receiver. The only thing left now was to take one more step forward and come into contact with the oddity of this certain presence. To keep the idea of this presence from driving him insane he imagined various possibilities, trying to prepare himself for the excitement of this new, imminent world.

Even so, his excitement refused to abate, as if all his preparations had been in vain; this was, for better or worse, due to the extraordinary nature of the aforementioned signal from another planet. The lifespan of the planet inhabited by the sender of the strange warning message had apparently been reduced to only ten minutes. Ten minutes from now that planet would be vaporized. This was a great surprise to him. But a moment later, he realized the absurdity of the situation and nearly broke out laughing—until further consideration kept him silent, listening intently to the mysterious planet's transmission.

The voice continued.

...Perhaps stating that this planet will evaporate into nothingness calls my sanity into question, but this broadcast bearing my last words could not be more sincere. Ah, my final broadcast! I myself realize how extraordinary such a declaration is, yet I feel the most effective way to leave behind these last words is to transform them into radio waves and broadcast them to all corners of this vast universe. Even were I to write something on paper or carve it into a stone, you would surely see the futility of these actions if you consider that ten minutes from now, the very world encompassing that paper or stone would be reduced to dust scattering throughout the reaches of space. Nevertheless, plans must be made to preserve, or at least communicate my last words to a distant planet. With our limited intellect, we know only that electromagnetic waves with a short wavelength can escape beyond the surface of our world and traverse the vast universe towards countless other planets.

However, I still have doubts that these last words will actually be understood by some lifeform on another planet. For instance, there is the uncertainty about whether the limited transmission power available to me will ultimately be able to produce a signal sufficiently strong to carry a message to every corner of this great universe. I have chosen the short wavelength of sixteen meters (whose message is least likely to be interrupted during transmission), but I fear it will be unable to cross the entire 400 billion light-years of our universe. Even assuming that the signal carrying my message safely reaches a planet, I am skeptical as to whether the beings living there will truly be able to comprehend the ideas of my people. As I brood over these things my worries only multiply, and my courage to carry out this final broadcast dwindles to nothing.

Nonetheless, the reason I am now attempting this unreliable experiment—a transmission whose futility can be compared to letting loose an arrow into an infinite, bottomless well—is because, after all, my life will end in only ten minutes (or rather, at this point I have but nine minutes remaining, alas!), and also because of the unbearable fact that the planet I inhabit will be destroyed without a trace, a highly remarkable history and culture built up over eight billion years lost in its entirety forever, without even a speck of dust left. How can I keep quiet about this? Thinking about all this makes me lightheaded. My mind, for which I always had a modicum of pride in when standing before the podium in physics class, is numb as if from repeated blows. Oh, I only have nine minutes left to live...I fear I may have already lost my sanity.

I must devote the few remaining minutes to this cursed final broadcast. But there is more! There is a very important reason I must continue this effort up until the moment of my death. Of the several hundred million people living on this planet, I am the only one who believes the end of the world is a mere nine minutes away. A great number of people—every soul with the exception of me—is unaware of their fated curse drawing so near. Furthermore, if their own ignorance prevents them from discerning the truth, perhaps I can show a gentle compassion for them. But on second thought, no, I can no longer bear to have such a stylish compassion for these people. Put simply, their lack of awareness stems from a repugnant coercion and a regrettable blindness to logic. To state things more blatantly, the hedonistic public (ignorant by nature) has been thoroughly deceived by the remorseless, cowardly actions of a group of scholars opposing my aforementioned Armageddon theory, and the public's self-induced hypnosis has only made things worse. Then, losing all self-control in a state akin to a drunken stupor, they rallied below the evil swords of the opposing scholars and swarmed at me like a massive overflowing river assailing a straw house, insulting my honor and robbing me of my happiness. To make matters worse, they even crushed my left eye and broke my arm, two things that should have no bearing on their interests.

The newspapers dramatized my actions with headlines like "Traitor to Humanity" and "Disruptor of Peace." Some even went as far as issuing a special edition with the large title, "Send him to the gallows at once!" The police sent a mental institution transport bus to pick me up and concentrated two divisions of soldiers and 3,000 police officers along the road to control the wild crowd clamoring for my execution. Had I not known the technique of seeking pity from cowardly women and maidservants of old friends, I would probably never have reached the point where I can move around freely like this (notwithstanding that I now reside in a cellar). What was it that perturbed them all? Of course, it was nothing more than the success of the opposing scholars' prescribed plan. Nonetheless, they must have been quite irritated upon reading my warning in the newspaper that only ten days remained until they would all be destroyed in one fell swoop. I've done my best to use theory to provide a sufficient explanation. I published my findings across thirteen types of media, including popular magazine articles. I even took part in a debate in a college lecture hall. Yet there was nothing but jeers and laughs, without even a single person able to understand me to any meaningful extent. Particularly regrettable were the shallow conjectures of a group of domain experts who happened to be my colleagues. I'll never forget what happened that day. In a certain college in the capital I had scheduled the first lecture of a series titled, "The Theory of Imminent Armageddon." I had been strongly advised beforehand to cancel the lecture, but because I had made a commitment I flatly refused this advice and held it anyway. My lecture that day went something like this.

I cordially consider it the greatest possible honor to be permitted, despite my inadequate knowledge and ability, to stand here today before this crowd of renowned academic authorities and present my theory, which I have named "The Theory of Imminent Armageddon."

Before moving on to my main topic, I hope you will allow me to speak a few words regarding the maxim "Thou shalt revere God." Our race represents the most advanced form of life on this planet, and ever since our first appearance on this land approximately 50,000 years ago we have utilized our intellect to wholly satisfy our desires.

However, because there is no limit to our desires—and because in recent times these desires have become so easy to fulfill—we have, out of necessity, reached the point where some of our desires as a people require a heavy dose of prudence. From one perspective this can be seen as an unavoidable situation, but at the same time it can be viewed as a terrible trap. We, as a race, must at all times maintain a proper reverence. I believe that at all costs we must refrain from forgetting our reverence for God and committing profane acts. Nevertheless, I feel that in the modern age we have savagely smashed through the generous boundaries established for us and let our desires become increasingly irreverent towards God.

For example, I find the scheming and greed around the acquisition of the 95th element *chrorium*—the so-called "wonder drug" we have at last discovered after 50,000 years—to be particularly disgraceful. Immediately following the discovery that taking this substance in sufficient doses would achieve the long-sought goal of immortality, unsightly conflict broke out throughout the globe as everyone rushed to get hold of this extremely scarce element. Chrorium, even rarer than radium, only exists in quantities enough for a few people (assuming a normal method of distribution) and can't possibly satisfy the demand of our entire race. Because of this, eventually a massive amount of money was spent on researching a way to produce synthetic chrorium.

The most promising method discovered to produce vast quantities of chrorium involves a special technique to convert eighteen atoms of oxygen into a single atom of chrorium. I believe a few of you in attendance here today are familiar with the details of this process.

But before attempting such an endeavor, I think we must carefully consider two things. First, is it truly a good thing to condone sparking a desire for eternal life in all members of our race? Furthermore, can experiments to transform oxygen to chromium actually be carried out safely? I would like to state emphatically that both of these concerns are extremely harmful to each and every one of us.

Above all, it would be an unforgivable sin for each of us God-created beings to consume chrorium procured by pushing aside others in our lust for immortality, undoubtedly triggering atrocious behavior—such as families tearing themselves apart—as society's morals degrade below those of lower-order animals. We must exercise self-control to avoid such a situation at all costs.

Second of all, I can assert with certainty that experiments to transform oxygen gas into chrorium have an ample risk of causing a disaster of the worst possible proportions. I implore you to listen to my observations on this topic, the central point of my discussion, in the form of a new theory that is founded on physics, my area of expertise.

Through many years of molecular physics research I have developed a theory related to the mysterious connection between hydrogen and helium. As you all know, hydrogen's structure is the simplest of all matter, composed of a single proton forming the nucleus around which revolves a single electron.

Furthermore, after hydrogen, helium atoms have the second simplest structure: two electrons revolving around a central nucleus made from a cluster of four protons and two more electrons. The weight of a helium atom is equivalent to four, and this is where the mystery lies.

A hydrogen atom consists of a single proton-electron pair, and if you add them up you'll see that a helium atom is composed of exactly four proton/electron pairs, hence helium's weight should naturally be four times that of hydrogen.

However, multiplying the weight of a hydrogen atom, 1.008, by four results in 4.032, a value that is 0.032 greater than helium's actual weight of four. I contemplated why these were not equivalent and realized that helium had become lighter because, unlike hydrogen where a proton-electron pair moved independently, it had a nucleus where four protons were lumped together with two electrons. In other words, when four hydrogen atoms become a single helium atom, the weight is reduced by 0.032.

When I thought about how this 0.032 of weight might vanish, I realized that it was in fact converted to energy. From the theory of relativity, I knew that the weight of all matter could be converted into the power to do a certain amount of work, for instance electrical power or mechanical power, what I am simply referring to here as *energy*.

Working through the calculations, if we assume that one gram of hydrogen is converted completely into helium, a terribly massive amount of electrical energy will be produced, equivalent to the work of 134,000 horsepower for one hour. Seventy speed trains can be powered at once just by converting a single gram of hydrogen into helium, so there is undoubtedly an enormous amount of energy created.

Now, to take a step back from that horrifying truth, in the experiment that is about to be attempted, the conversion of oxygen to chrorium, the amount of energy that is created when one gram of oxygen is made into an amount of chromium the size of a flea's eyeball is approximately 100,000 times the energy of when hydrogen is made into helium; this can be expressed as 13.1 billion horsepower, a demonically massive amount of power that we cannot even begin to conceive of. From what I have heard, the experiment about to be undertaken by some of you here will involve 7,000 grams of oxygen, leading to an immense amount of energy generated at its completion. This is enough to give me cerebral anemia just by thinking about it.

I am terrified to consider what will happen when such an enormous amount of energy is released in a burst. I severely doubt that this astonishing magnitude of energy can be easily controlled by us.

I can envision it now...Oh no, this will be the beginning of the worst possible disaster. This massive energy, released in such a small area in such a small span of time, will transcend the power of our people and trample our very souls. I believe that soon after, a secondary and tertiary atomic transformation will occur, followed by a 4th-order and 5th-order one, with the endlessly expanding atomic transformation triggering many thousands of earthquakes, tornadoes, and storms to assault our world—resulting in a chaos of collision, heat, ruin, evaporation, and dispersion while our beloved planet is destroyed in the blink of an eye.

At this point in my lecture, the professors sitting in the first row who were in charge of the experiment to produce chrorium all stood up, faces flushed scarlet and arms flailing wildly above their heads. The confusion that followed requires no explanation. A professor next to me shouted things like, "You should be expelled at once from the physics community for forgetting Newton's laws!" and, "How do you account for the eternal law of energy conservation?" To this day I vividly remember one professor's hate-filled expression. The next moment a mob rushed towards me like a giant wave, and I blacked out. It was then that I lost one arm along with my left eye. Oh no, there's only 30 seconds left! 28 seconds, 26 seconds...

The time of judgment has come. Who will prove to be right: me or those fools? Oh, I'm about to faint...The moment draws near when those half-wit college professors flip the switch of their irreverent experiment. Ten seconds left. I will never give up, never! These are my final words—

now carry away my weary soul! Ahh...three seconds. Damn you all! Two seconds, one...

Pressed tightly against the receiver's panel, Yukichi Amano's face dripped sweat, while his headphone-covered ears burned a bright red, as if about to melt.

After he heard the end of the ill-fated countdown, "Two seconds, one..." the final broadcast from an unknown race of people inhabiting a strange planet suddenly went silent. Yukichi was extremely tense, every nerve in his body on edge as he strained to listen for even the smallest sound.

But the silence stretched on, punctuated only by occasional cracks and pops.

Well, they actually did it. That man's planet must have just vaporized into mist, with all of the opposing scientists...and the rest of the people...

But the instant this thought popped into Yukichi's mind, something happened.

He saw a blindingly bright light a moment before the girder directly above his head snapped in two and came crashing down, crushing him. There was a sound like a gas tank exploding and a twelve-story building collapsing, a cacophony of creaks and shaking. With a terrible cracking sound, an unknown fate befell him.

A moment later he let out a terrible groan. Just as a searing pain cut through his back and legs, Yukichi became aware of random fragments of objects flying before his eyes.

He suddenly had a realization.

"Dammit!" he screamed (or would have, had he been able to).

It had been a terrible mistake to think that things were over with the destruction of the planet sending the man's final broadcast. There was no limit to the fiercely accelerating destruction; the infinite energy created by the planet's annihilation spread to another planet, which was, in turn, destroyed itself, scattered to pieces in an instant as the wave of destruction further accelerated...Oh no, the universe will be laid to ruin. This entire vast universe will be destroyed. The stampede of destruction will not rest until every last bit of the universe, even the tiniest meteorite, is vaporized to nothing.

But just as Yukichi, half-conscious, envisioned the universe returning to a state of utter silence and transparency, like staring at an empty glass jar lacking even a single spec of dust, the other half of his consciousness winked out, never to return.

The next morning, a Tokyo newspaper ran two large, dramatic news headlines side by side on page five:

Man arrested by Ministry of Communications last night for running unlicensed VHF broadcast

In freak accident, Shirakawa Flight School airplane on night training flight crashes into private residence, destroying roof and violently killing Yukichi Amano (24) performing radio research in his attic

Poor Yukichi never knew what hit him. He was, without a doubt, better off that way.

ADVENTURES OF THE DINOSAUR-CRAFT

Two Boys

Hello everyone. I'd like to introduce to you Jimmy and Sam.
 I'm certain that you will all enjoy hearing about the wonderful adventures of these two boys traveling to a tropical archipelago for their summer break.

Well then, let's have Jimmy begin the story.

Oh, and one more thing. Please gather around, but don't forget your handkerchief. Because as you listen to this story, you may find warm perspiration coating your palms, or cold, sticky sweat oozing down your back. But that's not all. You may even discover sweat on your belly button!

OK, Jimmy. You can take the floor...

Off to a tropical archipelago! There's nothing more boring than summer break.

Our friend Sam shares my opinion on this matter.

Right around the time when summer break was five weeks away, Sam and I felt a great shudder of horror, horrific enough to make each and every one of our hairs stand on end.

Sam and I had discussions every day about what we could do to escape from the terrible boredom of summer break.

As a result, we finally managed to catch hold of a wonderful idea: instead of what we normally did during summer break, this time we would venture to some deserted island. We felt that an archipelago somewhere in the tropics would probably be a good place.

At school we had learned about archipelagos in the tropics. Scorching sun, blue sea, white coral, red roofs, green jungles, colorful schools of fish; bananas, papayas, soursop, mangosteen, sea turtles, lizards, alligators, dark blue snakes (well, we weren't too interested in these); coconut trees, mangrove trees, rubber trees; heavy storms, malaria, dengue virus, a long boat called a "dugout," volcanoes, poisoned arrows...oh boy, they have it all. But I think I'll stop here.

Anyway...tropical archipelagos, aren't they just wonderful!

"Yeah, let's go."

"That decides it. Let's go!"

As Sam and I talked, flipping through the pages of an atlas of tropical regions, we became utterly fascinated with tropical archipelagos. We wished we could go to one tomorrow.

Both of us were impatient. After all, there were still over four weeks left until summer break.

"Oh, there's a really long time until summer break. I'm so bored."

"It's such a hot year that they should just start summer break one week early, don't you think?"

Sam and I just said whatever we wanted without really thinking about it.

However, our days before departing we weren't actually that boring. That was because we had so many things to do to prepare for spending sixty days in the tropics.

At last the first day of summer break came around, and we left on an airboat. Ahh, it was the start of a wonderful adventure!

Airboats are really wonderful, you know? We have friends that criticize Sam and me for constantly saying "wonderful," but we experience nothing but truly wonderful things, so we can only describe them as "wonderful." Anyway, when the boat was taking off it zipped across the water at an amazing speed. Waves formed and splashed onto the boat's windows. White waves washed over the windows, blocking the view of outside. The engine was running at a fierce speed, making a deafening sound as the boat went along. The airboat felt as if it was about to rip apart at any moment. Then the deafening sound suddenly stopped and there was silence. The fog on the windows cleared up, and the scenery outside became visible. That was the moment the airboat left the water.

I really love those few moments between when the airboat begins to accelerate until it separates from the water's surface. In particular, I can't put into words the amazing feeling I had the instant the boat took to the air. Oops, I'm supposed to be talking about our adventure in the tropics but I'm going on about an airboat. Let's get back to the main subject.

In only two days, that airboat carried us to the tropical archipelago of our desires. There we entered a tiny town by the name of Gineta.

Gineta was a little town with a population of only 8,000 people. Even so, it was the largest town in this tropical archipelago. Previously there was a government building with a governor-general. But no longer. You see, there are three volcanoes right next to the town and one of them erupted, spraying volcanic ash everywhere, not to mention the earthquakes, and sometimes there was a loud explosion when a great pillar fire shot up into the heavens; all this caused concern about having a government office in such a dangerous, unstable area, and so it was moved somewhere else.

Sam and I ended up staying in a place in this town called "The World Hotel." This hotel had a dramatic name, but in reality it was little more than an expanded run-down shack. However, there was one thing there that was quite nice: the basement. You could stand up inside and not bump your head on the ceiling.

The basement was built this way because the temperature in this region was very hot, and without such a basement the heat would radiate up from the ground and make the rooms uncomfortable.

But even with the basement, Sam and I were still hot and couldn't hang around inside the hotel. So we soon headed out to see the city.

In the city they sold various items—shells, coral, birds-of-paradise specimens, large stuffed lizards, beautifully polished turtle shells—and we wanted them all.

Sam was about to buy up all the souvenirs in a certain store. But I convinced him to first just look at the souvenirs, and after walking around and seeing everything to wait until tomorrow until buying anything, when he would start with those items he wanted the most. Sam grudgingly agreed to this.

But when Sam and I went out to the beach, I myself ended up breaking the very rule that I had just told him, for I found something which I deeply desired. But I wasn't the only one who wanted it. Sam too saw how inexpensive this item was and got excited about buying it even more than me. There were a bunch of them laying on the beach, small submarines, bean-shaped ones that could be operated by two people.

According to the seller, these tiny submarines were frequently used in this area in the past. However, the country that had made use of them lost a war and escaped, leaving many of the vehicles behind. After that, the submarines were put up for auction, but they didn't sell for lack of buyers. After many auctions, the entire group of them was finally bought by someone, apparently for an unbelievably low price.

The seller told us this, so it must be true. Furthermore, when we looked at the price tag attached to them, the price was indeed very inexpensive. We could buy one of these submarines using the same amount of money that would get us an electric model train, rail, and traffic lights. These submarines were practically free.

"Jimmy, let's get one of these."

"Yeah, that's a good idea."

I think at that time Sam and I both had our eyes wide open and rolling in circles in utter shock. Our bodies must have been trembling from the joy of finding something we really wanted.

So we bought it!

One bean-shaped mini submarine. We finally bought it!

A Wonderful Plan

We spent some time attending the Gineta nautical school to learn how to pilot our "Mini Submarine Dinosaur Craft" (don't you think that's a wonderful name?). Engineer Amir was formerly an officer in the navy for eight years and was very skilled at teaching us how to operate the submarine.

"Now boys, there's nothing to operating a craft like this. Just forget you're human and swim around like crazy, as if you've become a fish. See, like this..."

Amil showed us how he quickly submerged the submarine into the water and then immediately rose up to the surface, just like he was swimming.

"However, there is one thing you must never forget. When submerging, always make sure you check that the hatch on the upper deck is properly closed. Are you following me?"

"Yes. We are listening."

"And one more thing when you are going underwater. Be sure there is nothing on the upper deck that would cause a problem if submerged in water."

"What do you mean, 'cause a problem if submerged in water'?"

"I'll give you an example to make it easy for you to understand. For instance, let's say a person remained on the upper deck. If you forget about them and the ship submerges into the ocean, that person would be in serious trouble, wouldn't they? Although I guess rather than be in trouble they would simply drown."

"Oh, that makes sense..."

"Second example. Let's say you are drying some flour out in the sun that has been infested with bugs. If you forget to put that inside and the submarine submerges, you better say *sayonara* to that flour."

"Alright, we understand."

We tried our best to learn the submarine's operation, and Amil gave us the highest of praises for our enthusiasm.

There was a reason for our great enthusiasm: after obtaining the submarine, Sam and I thought of a wonderful plan. In order to carry out this plan to the best of our abilities we had to be skilled pilots of the mini submarine.

So what do you think our special plan was?

I think now it's time for us to reveal it. Our plan was, you see, to use the submarine to put a dinosaur in the ocean.

A dinosaur! Surely no one here doesn't know what that is.

Dinosaurs, giant reptiles that roamed the Earth many thousands of years ago. Dinosaurs, amazing beasts that span over thirty meters from head to tail. Dinosaurs, creatures that appeared in a village at the base of the Himalayas and terrified people. Dinosaurs, extending their long lizard necks and puffing out their chests as they suddenly mount a train. And don't forget that primeval monster of a dinosaur that was seen by people unexpectedly poking its neck out of the Loch Ness Lake in Scotland! Our plan was to use the mini submarine to make a dinosaur like that.

"How in the world can you do something like that?" you ask? Well, we can *definitely* do that. It's something that Sam and I devised after a great deal of thought.

We'll share the details about our contrivance with all of you. It goes like this: on the submarine we talked about there was a mast. Our plan was to put a fake dinosaur head on the top of the mast. Of course, we had to construct it using materials that could withstand water without deforming or discoloring.

Once we do this, we will make the submarine rise up off the ocean floor and then suddenly take it down again. But if we do this, what do you think will happen? It would likely appear as if a giant dinosaur was raising and lowering its head in and out of the ocean. Now if a steamboat just happened to be passing by, what would happen?

Oh no, a dinosaur has appeared next to our boat. Th-th-this is terrible!

A great uproar would break out upon the steamboat, the crew broadcasting over the radio, "The greatest mystery of the 20th century—a giant dinosaur has appeared in a tropical sea!" causing a terrible panic throughout the world.

With a camera installed in one of the dinosaur's eyes we would take many pictures of the confusion occurring aboard the steamboat. Then we would pretend nothing happened for a while. Once summer break was over, we would release those photographs, calling the collection "The Adventures of the Dinosaur-Craft," and make the entire world roar with laughter. In all honesty, this was the entirety of the big plan that Sam and I devised.

We designed the dinosaur's head that was needed for this plan and ordered its construction back at home via airmail. For some time I had known of a factory that manufactured such things. A reply came immediately from the factory, saying that our order would be completed within a week and shipped to our location via airmail.

Sam and I exchanged glances and began dancing for joy on the spot.

The Dinosaur-Craft Departs

Ten days later we received the package containing our manufactured dinosaur head.

Fitting within a square-meter box, it was surprisingly small. We returned to our hotel room, locked the door, and opened up our secret box.

Inside was a dinosaur head of excellent craftsmanship. It was just as we expected from that factory, but was manufactured far simpler, far more superior, and far easier to use than our design had specified.

The material comprising the dinosaur head was a finely woven chain netting. On top of that was a cover apparently made of some kind of waterproof silk, colored the same as the dinosaur's skin with holes for the eyes and mouth. When folded, the head fit easily into a small one meter-sized box; but when removed and inflated, it became quite large.

A camera was installed inside one of the dinosaur's eyes. In addition, while this wasn't part of my design, there was a mechanism for moving the dinosaur's head up, down, left, or right. With several chains hanging down this was the same mechanism used in a puppet, and the attached note said that all was required was winding and unwinding a crank that was attached to a pulley, so we should thread the chains through the mast and into the submarine.

There was suddenly a knock at the door.

We weren't concerned because the door was locked, but it suddenly opened with a loud noise and the bellhop entered.

The bellhop screamed out as he threw the sheets into the room and ran out.

"Darn it. He saw us."

"But you locked the door, right?"

"Yes, I definitely locked it. Oh boy, this isn't going to work. The door is slightly offset from the frame, so even if we lock it, the door will still open."

We hurried to put the dinosaur head back into the box. By the time the bellboy nervously brought the manager to our room, we had stored the head away completely. We sent them away, saying that the bellboy must have come here while sleepwalking and having a dream about seeing a monster.

However, after this happened we couldn't keep this package in the hotel for very long. So that night we carried it to our submarine that was parked at the pier of the Gineta nautical school on the coast. Unfortunately the moon wasn't out; it would only come out later in the night.

That night we slept in the mini submarine.

We woke up at 3 a.m., two hours before dawn. The half-moon was high in the sky. Aided by the moonlight, we attached the dinosaur head to the submarine's mast.

With only thirty minutes remaining before dawn, we tightly closed the dinosaur-craft's hatch and left the dock, submerging immediately. Once we got far out into the ocean we rose to the surface.

We took turns acting as the captain and the lookout. First Sam was the captain, and I was the lookout.

The lookout watched 360 degrees all around the horizon, checking if any boat was approaching. In addition, he occasionally glanced at the sky, checking for aircraft. We thought we wouldn't be able to surprise airplanes; it would only work with boats. The moment we saw a boat, we would submerge. Our plan was to suddenly pop up to the surface when the boat finally began to approach us.

On the first day, we didn't find much. After all, the city of Gineta wasn't particularly popular, so it wasn't rare to have days when not even a single boat entered or exited the port. That's why we tried waiting in the ocean outside of the port, but on that day no prey ever came.

"We weren't very lucky today," I told Sam after we got home.

He pulled a chart out of his bag and spread it out on the desk as he spoke.

"At that place we went to today, we'll never catch anything. But if we head out thirty miles to sea, we'll come to a major sea route. In other words, right here. If we wait somewhere on this route, I think a pretty big steamboat will eventually pass by. Thirty miles roundtrip will be a bit difficult, but do you want to try it tomorrow?"

"Hmm. Yeah, let's try," I said, and the next day we ran the engine at full throttle as we headed out deep.

From the exposure to the sun yesterday acting as lookouts, both Sam and I had gotten quite sunburned, and our skin was blackened.

"I guess today is not going very well either," I said.

"No, we just have to bide our time. It's not like all the world's boats are going to come here for us, so we just need to have more patience," said Sam, speaking like an adult.

However, later even he seemed discouraged, and on the way home said, "The stores are not open yet, so as soon as we see anything, even a tiny boat, let's scare the heck out of them."

"Yeah, that'll be great. Alright, let's find the first sacrificial ship!"

I took my position as the lookout.

When about three miles were remaining to the port, we caught sight of a group of five or six small wooden boats with sails. They were locals who had finished a day of fishing and were on their way back to the port.

"I found something. It's a fleet of six boats!"

"What? A fleet of six boats? Look closely. Isn't it a naval fleet? If we scare a naval fleet we'll be blasted to bits by rockets and cannons."

Sam was clearly worried.

"I gave them a good look. It's a fleet of six boats, however..."

" 'However'? What's the problem?"

"They're small local dugouts with their sails raised."

"What, small local dugouts? It won't be much of a show to scare them, but since the stores are opening now let's do it."

We executed the aforementioned plan. We immediately submerged the dinosaur-craft and began chasing after the fleet of boats. Then we suddenly raised the submarine to the surface. The dinosaur reared its terrifying head and stared down the local people's boats as it swayed from side to side.

Splash, splash. Thud, thud.

Screams rang out.

There was quite an uproar. The locals tossed aside their oars and jumped into the ocean in a frenzy.

We watched it all happen through the periscope and laughed so hard we couldn't stop crying.

We were afraid that if we showed the dragon for too long people would see through our ruse, so we soon took the submarine back down.

Revenge for a Prank

It was the following day when we encountered a large steamboat, *The Gloria.*

"Woah. It's coming, it's coming! A giant steamboat is coming this way! That massive vessel must be over 10,000 gross tons."

Sam, on lookout at the time, raised his voice to a great pitch. We immediately transitioned to underwater operations.

After that we just watched via the periscope.

The great vessel approached us, seemingly unaware of what lay in wait.

"Hey, Sam. That steamboat probably has a good telescope, so we should surface a distance away and not approach too closely."

"Yeah. But if there is too much distance between us, then they may not realize the dinosaur's existence. I guess we should have brought some fireworks."

"You think a dinosaur would launch fireworks?"

Eventually the dinosaur-craft cut across *The Gloria's* course. We were a half a mile from them. At this distance, they would realize our presence, whether they wanted to or not.

We carefully poked the dinosaur above the surface of the sea while moving its head back and forth. We also opened and closed the mouth.

This worked to great effect. Through our periscope we observed passengers and crew running around in a panic on the ship's deck.

"Ha, ha, ha. I wonder if they really don't realize it's a fake dinosaur. Even the captain seems to be panicking."

"Oh wow, they've started changing their course. It looks like they intend to escape."

As the vessel changed course its large belly turned to face us, kicking up a wave of white. The boat's hurried reaction and the panic of the crew and passengers was captured on our camera. Moments later the boat's backside was visible as it moved away at full speed.

We clapped our hands, slapped our knees, and rolled around laughing on the floor.

After that, the dinosaur-craft headed back to Gineta. However, the sun was still high in the sky, so it wasn't a good idea to return to the harbor yet. So Sam and I talked, and we decided to moor the submarine on a tiny uninhabited island seven miles away from Gineta and rest there until evening. A dense mangrove forest grew there all the way up to the shore such that if we hid in the shadows, there was no fear of the dinosaur's tall head being seen protruding up from the sea.

I'm glad that we quickly hid in the shadows of that uninhabited island, because only moments later several airplanes zipped by above us in the sky, making a terrific sound. My guess is that the massive steamboat from earlier was shocked by seeing our dinosaur and broadcast about it over the radio, asking for assistance, and this resulted in rescue airplanes flying here from all over to perform a search from the sky.

Airplanes flew by one after another as they surveyed the ground. The size of the planes gradually grew over time.

"There isn't much we can do. Those planes are still looking down on us."

"This isn't good. It's nearly nightfall. We haven't learned how to navigate at night, so we won't be able to move this thing until tomorrow morning."

"In that case, let's stay here tonight."

We stayed overnight in the shade of the uninhabited island. The airplanes continued their search into the night. Some of the planes were kind enough to drop flares as they passed.

"This has all turned into quite a big deal."

"I bet that the dinosaur sighting has made news throughout the world and everyone's making a fuss about it."

"That makes me really happy. But there's an uncomfortable number of mosquitoes here."

The sky began to gradually brighten.

Thinking we should go home soon, I listened carefully to the sounds around us. But a moment later I heard what sounded like the quiet buzz of an airplane.

"No luck. The planes are still busy in the air."

"Once dawn breaks, it's going to be hard for us to leave here. We're in trouble."

Morning came. The number of planes increased. Now it was even more difficult for us to move the submarine.

We stayed there that night and were forced to stay the next as well. The problem was food; we regretted not bringing more with us. Our water was completely exhausted. We disembarked and managed to satisfy our thirst by drinking the foul-smelling water from coconuts.

Dinosaur Sighting

On the morning of the fourth day, we woke up and went outside the submarine to find that there were fortunately no more airplane sounds.

"Alright, let's set sail soon. But before that, we need to gather ten coconuts and carry them into the submarine. We don't know what else is going to happen on this trip, so we should have enough water prepared."

"That's reasonable. Well then, each of us should gather five coconuts. Let's go."

Sam and I hurried onto the island. We entered a nearby forest of coconut trees and started gathering the coconuts that were the least ripe.

Each of us barely managed to hold five coconuts with two hands. Sam and I grunted as we left the forest and staggered towards the bay where our submarine was docked.

Right at that moment Sam stood up and said, "What the..."

"What's wrong Sam?" I asked.

"Hmm. It seems something is wrong with my eyes. I see two dragon heads."

"What are you talking about?" I laughed and looked towards the bay, thinking Sam was acting strange.

"Oh no!"

The coconuts dropped from my arms onto the ground. My knees suddenly started to tremble, my throat became dry, and I was unable to speak. Why, you ask? Well, because I saw *it*. Next to our dinosaur was another dinosaur sticking out its long neck, opening and closing its mouth with lumbered movements. At a glance it was clear this was no fake. The beast's large body crushed mangrove trees with a great crunching sound, and its long tail slapped the tops of coconut trees. I saw coconuts rolling around on the ground. This was a real dinosaur.

"Let's get out of here. It's a real dinosaur!"

Seeming to realize what was happening himself, Sam grabbed my arm. Without a sound I turned around and started running into the depths of the jungle.

"That sure was a surprise! There's actually a real dinosaur living on this island."

"There are actually still islands where dinosaurs roam. I wonder if that thing eats humans."

"Dinosaurs are reptiles, right? Snakes and lizards are examples of reptiles, and some snakes eat humans. Therefore, I think dinosaurs eat humans."

"What do you mean 'therefore'? If we get eaten it's game over. Oh, this is terrible!"

"More importantly, since our dinosaur-craft won't respond to anything that beast says I'm worried that it might get upset and crush us with its foot so that we'll sink to the bottom of the ocean."

"Oh, I just remembered something. I forgot to close the hatch. That's not good. But that real dinosaur will definitely get upset because our dinosaur is not answering back."

"If that happens, the vessel we were going to use to get home will be destroyed. Then we'll have no choice but to live on this island with the real dinosaur."

"Wow, just thinking about living together with a real dinosaur gives me the chills!"

Sam made a show of his entire body trembling.

"Hey, Sam. I wonder if this dinosaur has a good sense of smell. In other words, is it good at picking up certain scents?"

"Why would you ask something like that?"

"Because I was just thinking of quietly going out to the bay now to see what the real dinosaur is doing. But if it has a good sense of smell, as soon as we approach it'll discover us and we'll be eaten."

"That dinosaur probably has a pretty weak sense of smell. Because even though it was right next to our fake dinosaur, the real dinosaur hasn't realized yet that it's not real."

"Alright then, I'm going to go check."

"I'm going too."

Making as little noise as possible, we walked cautiously towards where we could see the bay.

"Hey, the dinosaur isn't there anymore."

"You're right. Let's quickly get into the dinosaur-craft and get out of here."

"Alright. Hurry!"

Now that I think about it, I have no memory of jumping into the dinosaur-craft, setting sail, or even who closed the hatch. I just know that we wanted to survive and tried to escape from there as quickly as possible and head deep out to sea. Of course we didn't submerge. We simply moved at full throttle across the surface of the water, kicking up white waves. We were in an utter state of panic, worried that the dinosaur was going to start following us at any moment...

"Whew, we made it!" we thought as we moored our vessel in the shallows of the Gineta bay. We jumped out of the submarine, crossed the water, and ran up to the sand where we fell unconscious, finally safe and sound.

We didn't know it at the time, but apparently people around that area were completely stupefied. But that's to be expected, because moments later they noticed a dinosaur rushing towards the shore at full speed, and when it reached the shallows two young boys burst out, only to collapse to the sand on their backs.

It seems even the people at the hotel, realizing we hadn't returned in three days, thought we must have been carried off by a dinosaur and split up to come search for us.

We were lucky enough to return to our home country in one piece. Sam and I had a really rough time, but we eventually broadcasted our stories of "The Adventures of the Dinosaur-Craft" and "The Time We Saw a Dinosaur." We even published a book about our experiences, becoming wealthy from the profits. For our next vacation I want to try going to Japan. I'll ask Sam one of these days what he thinks.

CREMATORIA

Yasosuke Kono

"Hmm..." detective author Yasosuke Kono shook his head doubtfully as he passed through the crowd filling the night market.

Truth be told, while Yasosuke Kono was formally an author of detective stories, he was in reality a perpetual amateur unable to achieve even a modicum of success. Writing stories generally required creative ideas. Detective stories in particular could not be written without fresh ideas. He had accepted a job from a certain magazine publisher, but at the time his dim-witted head didn't contain even a single good idea. Even if you turned him upside down, surely not even the tiniest creative idea would fall out. Driven by frustration, as usual he wandered out to the Shinjuku night market. Having the experience of once getting a great idea there, Yasosuke clung to the vain hope that he might have similar luck tonight.

"Well now...who was that guy..." he mumbled again to himself, turning up the collar of his overcoat against the chilly breeze.

In the midst of the crowd Yasosuke had just passed by a man he was certain of having met before. The man was quite an odd character, being unusually tall, yet hunched over and unnaturally gaunt. Below his eyes were thick dark circles, and the few fine wrinkles running along his cheeks somehow made him resemble a monkey. On his head was a brown scarf, the kind you would see worn by a master of some ancient art, but in contrast to that he wore a long,

Chinese-style overcoat that appeared to be made of silk. Holding a cane in his right hand, the man dragged one foot when he walked.

"Hey..." Yasosuke had called out to the unusual man. This was only natural, considering his unbearably shameless nature...

"Hellooo..." the man responded meekly, more wrinkles appearing around his mouth as he nodded his trembling head back and forth.

That was enough to satisfy Yasosuke, and he had no intention of saying anything else. From there he parted with this acquaintance and quickly returned to the crowd, heading towards Yotsuya Mitsuke.

(Who was that guy?)

Yasosuke felt excited at the prospect of remembering something about the man he had just exchanged words with. So without further ado he began this amusing diversion.

However, no matter how much he tried, not even a single detail about the man popped into his mind.

"Who was he? I have to remember something about him..."

Beginning with his elementary school years, Yasosuke searched for the unusual man in every period of his life up to now—his years at middle school, then college; his years of dating, followed by marriage; his years of dissipation after his wife died; and finally, his years as an author—but he was unable to uncover anything pertinent. Something was on the verge of surfacing, yet never did. A vague irritation began to gnaw at him.

Just then, he passed by a large display window. One of the news photographs there caught his attention: a picture of a general in imposing formal attire within a thick black frame, printed with the words, "The late General Ichinomiya." When Yasosuke glanced at the black frame, in a flash he realized who that unusual man was.

"Oh, it's him!" he cried out.

Yet, strangely enough, the moment his voice died down a shadow came over his face. *But why would that be?*

Senshiro Nezumiya

"Yes, it's him. It *must* be him!"

An old memory of Mantis Man flashed through his mind. Why did that happen when he looked at the black-framed picture? Perhaps you would call it a sixth sense, but it seemed so odd that he couldn't stop thinking about it. Regardless, when he finally solved the mystery days later, Yasosuke was so amazed that he caught his breath.

"Yes, his appearance is completely different, but it must be Senshiro Nezumiya!"

Senshiro Nezumiya. As Yasosuke repeated that name to himself he remembered those early, curiosity-filled days of elementary school. The very first time he sat before a shiny desk that smelled of fresh wood, right beside him was a shy boy named Senshiro Nezumiya. Back then Senshiro had a pasty complexion but was quite a handsome boy with big, bright eyes and pale, yet cute lips. Their desks just happened to be next to one another, so before he knew it the two boys became good friends. Their friendship only deepened with age, but once it came time to graduate from college they realized they would likely no longer be able to see each other daily, and the two caused a great commotion of the likes only possible by young men of that age.

In the end, Yasosuke and Senshiro thought of a great way to make things work. Around that time their places of employment had already been decided, with Yasosuke planning on commuting to an insurance company in Marunouchi, and Senshiro a certain cosmetics manufacturer in Tsukiji. So they agreed to meet at 5 p.m. at a cafe by the name of Zinnia on a backstreet in Ginza, roughly the same distance from their workplaces, where they would sip tea as they chatted about everything that happened that day. This was indeed a great idea; the young men grew quite merry and couldn't help laughing about that great commotion they caused during graduation.

However, while this rendezvous at Zinnia was undoubtedly a great idea, through some twist of fate an unexpected catastrophe came to befall their relationship. They were pulled apart by a young girl, as beautiful as a hydrangea blooming in the corner of a garden on an overcast day.

"Senshiro, he's kind and gentle, and I like him," Tsuyuko said to a coworker.

But then another day she said, "Yasosuke is such a cheerful boy. Unlike me, he's never struggled in life. How nice."

The two best friends were suddenly enemies as they rushed to win the love of Tsuyuko, but in the end it was Yasosuke who triumphed. Right around the time Yasosuke and Tsuyuko were delighting in the sweet taste of love as they started their new rose-colored family, Senshiro, having suffered every waking moment in the depths of despair, disappeared to an undisclosed location. Even Yasosuke and Tsuyuko couldn't help but catch wind of this. As expected, they grew concerned and even hired a detective agency to perform a search to the best of their ability, but Senshiro's whereabouts remained unknown. He probably had committed suicide out of heartbreak in a place where he would never be found—or so thought Yaosuke and Tsuyuko.

However, three years later Yaosuke heard a strange rumor: Senshiro Nezumiya was still alive. Furthermore, he was supposedly living under a roof in the very same city of Tokyo, breathing the same air as them. He was working as the head cremator in the Hanayama Crematorium.

During that time, even at work Yasosuke was distracted by thoughts of Senshiro and unable to get much done, but not only did Senshiro seem to have no intention to cause harm to the couple, but the next year he even sent them a typical New Year's card. As a result, before they knew it their initial feelings of surprise and concern dissipated. After one, two, three years passed, and then two more, Senshiro Nezumiya was to Yasosuke no more than a stranger. But there was another reason for that: Yasosuke's beloved wife Tsuyuko had suddenly passed away this spring from what at first seemed to be a minor illness, so he quickly forgot about the man he had fought for her love.

If Senshiro hadn't appeared before his eyes like this, Yasosuke surely would have never had another thought about the man again for the rest of his life...

"Hmm..." Yasosuke stood frozen on the sidewalk, seemingly in surprise. He had suddenly remembered something of critical importance that slipped his mind until this moment.

"Hmm...But Senshiro Nezumiya is supposed to be dead..."

Through the Darkness it Leapt

"There's no way Senshiro Nezumiya is still alive!"

Yasosuke's reaction was only natural, especially after having just remembered his reception of a postcard announcing Senshiro's death. How could such an important thing have slipped his mind?

He recalled reading a message along these lines:

"...We regret to respectfully announce that after failing to recover, Mr. Senshiro Nezumiya has at last fallen into an eternal sleep. On the forthcoming date listed below his Buddhist funeral ceremony will take place at the Hanayama service room, followed by cremation in the Hanayama Crematory..."

Judging from this, Senshiro had indeed died from illness, and his body was cremated. Not to mention the irony of him being cremated in the same place he had been in charge of before his death. While one cannot discount the possibility of a corpse reanimating in the middle of a funeral ceremony, causing a great uproar, surely that is an extremely rare event, and if such a thing were to occur there is no way a sharp-eyed newspaper reporter looking for a scoop would miss it. But judging from the fact that no recent newspapers had run such a cheerful story, Senshiro's body was undoubtedly transformed into ashes without a hitch and dispersed from the chimney of the crematorium. But that means...

It meant that in the night market crowd, Yasosuke had just seen none other than Senshiro Nezumiya's ghost.

"Ooohhhh..."

He began to shake uncontrollably and nervously adjusted the collar of his overcoat to cover his neck. After what he had just witnessed, this wasn't the time to fuss over ideas for a story. He felt stricken with a great feeling of anxiety, as if cerebral anemia was about to strike. And so he shoved open the door of a bar on the street and went inside.

"Get me some brandy...quickly, some brandy!"

Shouting at the young waitress, Yasosuke ordered Western liquor. The few moments it took until the shot glass was put before him felt like endless hours. He brushed aside the waitress as she tried to open the bottle, but instead opened it himself and poured it into the glass. Then he gulped down four or five shots of the overflowing liquid in quick succession. Yasosuke felt his stomach suddenly heat up, and soon a sensation like fire was expanding throughout his entire body.

"Ahh..." he sighed deeply.

"Yes, that was just what I needed!" he thought, then took hold of the glass once again. Yasosuke gradually calmed down until he took notice of the silence around him.

Just then, Yasosuke overheard the conversation of two men near his table who were talking quietly.

"That's why..." said the man in a short *haori* coat embroidered with a family crest. "What's strange is how, of all people, General Ichinomiya—a man who would never have played with stocks—sold all his property for cash right before he passed away, not to mention spent it all somewhere, with his family now claiming they barely have enough money for living expenses."

"What's also strange is the general's sudden death. I can't believe he would die so young."

"Once I saw a strange man at the general's residence. The guy was dragging one foot, his lanky body reminiscent of a sickly praying mantis. He must be playing a part in all this."

"But I thought he too was supposed to have died after that..."

At this point in the conversation, Yasosuke was unable to bear listening anymore. The man like a praying-mantis that they were talking about had to be Senshiro Nezumiya. These two were also saying he was supposed to be dead.

Yasosuke placed a silver coin upon the table and rushed out of the bar.

Ghost Man

Once Yasosuke left the bar, he found himself at the edge of a bustling night market. There were no stores open beyond this point, only a street that felt lonely, as if night had fallen without notice. He hurried ahead, no specific destination in mind.

At that moment, he heard a voice calling from behind.

"Yasosuke, can you hear me..."

Hearing his name unexpectedly called, Yasosuke froze in terror. *Don't look behind you*, someone seemed to be warning him. But who can resist turning around when their name is called?

"Can you hear me? Well, if it isn't Yasosuke..."

"Aghh!" he made up his mind and, mustering all his courage, turned around.

"What the..."

Standing there was a tall, lanky man, like a praying mantis with dark circles under his eyes: the ghost of Senshiro Nezumiya.

"Hey Yasosuke," said the monster with a big grin.

"Wh-who are you…"

"You don't know who I am? How disappointing…" said the monster without a trace of disappointment on his face. "It's Senshiro, the boy who sat at the desk beside you in middle school."

"Senshiro should have died some time ago."

"Well, if you knew that guy, it will make it easy for me to say this." He chuckled as he made this odd statement. "How could a dead person come back to life like this and speak to you? But if we put that question aside for the moment and assume such a thing is possible, don't you think it would be a truly amazing notion?"

"Don't be ridiculous. If you're really a ghost, then why don't you act like one?" But right after speaking Yasosuke grew annoyed at himself for being the ridiculous one.

"But in any case…leaving to your imagination whether I am a ghost, or a living human being, I have something to ask you."

For a ghost, Senshiro said some pretty reasonable things, and Yasosuke didn't know what to make of this. Nor could he think of what to say in response.

"Listen to me. I know you lost your wife. To be sure, you two had a very strong love for one another. You were the victor of a magnificent love…"

"W-why are you talking about this *now*?"

"Yes, well…and so what I want to ask you is about your departed wife, Tsuyuko. In particular, whether you might want to see her again."

"See Tsuyuko again?!"

It didn't matter if Yasosuke wanted to see her again; she was dead. Her body was cremated, and he brought back a tiny bit of her ashes that are now buried in Tama Cemetery. Trying to meet someone who had been turned into ashes was more difficult than splashing a bucketful of water onto the ground and then putting every drop back in the bucket. Besides being a ghost, it would be a gross understatement to say this mantis-man was unusual.

"Are you following me? A man who is supposed to be dead is now standing before you. Look around, this place is a bit quiet but it's definitely a street in Yotsuya. If you will acknowledge that I am alive now, then why don't you take a careful look around and consider that your beloved wife might still be alive."

Upon hearing this, with a start Yasosuke began carefully looking around the area where Senshiro was standing.

"As I expected, it seems you *are* curious," Senshiro chuckled again as he bared teeth stained black from tobacco.

Yasosuke blushed in embarrassment. But he was not able to find any sign of his deceased wife's ghost.

Strange Man, Strange Talk

Senshiro chuckled again. "No matter how much you search, you definitely won't find her here."

Senshiro's delight grew by the moment as Yasosuke's anger became more and more unbearable.

"You're just trying to tease me. Stop with the dirty tricks."

"You think I'm teasing you?" Senshiro made a dramatic show of being surprised. "That's quite an accusation. I'm being completely serious here. By not believing what I say, *you* are the one who is being rude...and yet, I think it's only natural for you to doubt me. What I am telling you is certainly quite extraordinary."

Senshiro looked upset for a moment, but his expression soon softened and he looked at Yasosuke consolingly. Yasosuske finally regained his composure, even as he realized he might be playing into Senshiro's trap...

"In any case, you've lied to everyone," Yasosuke said harshly, like a slap to the face. "You sent out a death notice even though you were still alive. If I had never come across you tonight, I probably would have continued to believe you were cremated and turned to ashes. Why did you fake your own death?"

"I didn't fake it. That death notice was real. Just calm down and listen to everything I have to say, for it's an utterly bizarre story of the likes you've never heard before..."

Senshiro grabbed hold of Yasosuke's arm and wouldn't let go. He said that he couldn't talk here, so they should go get a drink somewhere. Senshiro said he knew of a certain familiar bar nearby, and began to forcefully lead the hesitant Yasosuke there.

It was a bar on the backstreets of Shinjuku with the name of "Guillotine," but even though Yasosuke was familiar with that area, that night was the first time he heard of the place. When they pushed open the door and went inside, the dirt floor enclosed a large, gloomy space, and in the front was a cluster of shelves bearing a surprising variety of liquor bottles—labels in red, blue, and yellow— with the bar uncomfortably high, behind which stood a bartender facing away from them, somehow reminiscent of a wax figure.

"Welcome...your seats have been prepared over there."

Like a wind-up doll whose springs suddenly kicked into gear, the bartender raised a pale arm from under his coat and motioned towards a table in the corner. Upon it was a flower vase containing white roses. This bar was looking stranger and stranger. Yasosuke remembered once seeing a similar-looking house in a western painting of ghosts.

As soon as Senshiro ordered their cocktails he continued the conversation from earlier.

"...Are you listening to me, Yasosuke? For a time I did die and was put into the oven at Hanayama Crematory. There are many people who have witnessed that. For them, I think it will be easier to believe I'm dead rather than alive. Because I truly did die. I went to the land of the dead, and then returned to this world. Now you mustn't misunderstand me. I'm probably clearly visible to you, but I've long ago ceased being a member of this world."

"How ridiculous. Stop with this nonsense. Who in their right mind would think you were a man from the land of the dead? Anyway, let's have a drink to celebrate you being alive."

Yasosuke thought there was definitely something wrong with Senshiro, so he offered a toast in order to get away from him as quickly as possible.

"You're offering a toast to me? How kind of you. Well then..."

They clinked together their glasses, then each gulped down their drink.

"Ahh, I've finally done it. Now let's drink a toast to you, my friend," Senshiro said as he signaled to the bartender.

"Finally done it? What are you talking about?" Yasosuke challenged Senshiro.

"That's my secret for now. But you'll understand soon enough. Because I have confidence you'll believe my claim that I'm not from this world...All right, our drinks are here. Here's to you."

"What? You are..."

Yasosuke stopped mid-sentence as he felt the alcohol begin to take effect. It was like the entire world before him—the bar, Senshiro, and everything else—had abruptly receded into the distance.

(No...I must stay awake...)

He tried to support himself with his hands, but Yasosuke's upper body doubled over against his will and collapsed hard onto the table.

Goldfish in the Flames

Yasosuke was in the middle of a strange dream.

Whirr...whirr...whirr...

He was dangling somewhere in space where an unusual noise droned on. There was the sensation of bathing in a sea of flickering neon lights colored red, or perhaps green.

Whirr...whirr...whirr...

Ripples that seemed to form a complex pattern washed towards him at regular intervals, flowing over his body and then away. Approaching from the left and the right, up and down, and even front and back (when contemplating this at a later time, he found it odd that he could even see clearly behind him) were beautiful rainbows, flying straight like javelins that passed dangerously close to his body. Soon those too evaporated like foam on the ocean, only to be replaced by schools of soap bubbles of various sizes floating up here and there.

Whirr...whirr...whirr...

The large groups of bubbles ascended as they jiggled back and forth, seeming to rise up infinitely, but eventually the topmost bubbles suddenly halted, as if on command; their movement suggested that bubbles had struck some invisible ceiling. The bubbles that continued rising from below began to clump up and quickly bounced off one another. Yasosuke felt a painful tightening sensation in his chest.

After that, as if blown by a strong wind the bubbles gradually began to stir, and a moment later began rotating. Their spinning quickly picked up speed until they were like vortexes, shapes dissolving until all that remained was dull grayish lights. Yasosuke's progressively darkening vision led to mounting feelings of uncertainty.

Just then, in the middle of the muddy jumble something suddenly twinkled. As he gazed intently, wondering what it might be, a single round glass object emerged. It was shaped like one of the glass fishbowls for goldfish sold at the night market, but it contained nothing.

(Is that a goldfish bowl?)

But just as he was thinking that, a flame erupted from the bottom of the bowl. Bright red tongues of flame rose up vigorously out of the goldfish bowl like you would see on an old picture of a fireball. Yasosuke could only stare in shock, gripped by an uncontrollable fear.

All of a sudden, the flame began moving upwards; inside the goldfish bowl the fire had flared up. As he watched, the base of the fire became visible and the flames quickly rose higher and higher. Soon the flames had risen to cover the entire upper opening of the glass bowl. Yasosuke looked closely, wondering what was below the flame, when he noticed the clear surface of water.

The water had a pale blue tint to it, perhaps because of the glass, that rippled now and then. There were glimpses of red objects that momentarily appeared between the ripples.

(What are those?)

The number of red specks of light gradually increased. On closer inspection, Yasosuke saw that they were goldfish.

(There's goldfish swimming in there!)

Cute little goldfish were swimming around, what a bizarre sight indeed! Immediately above the fish's heads was the surface of the water, but right next to it burned the terrible red hot flames. Yasosuke gazed with pity at the poor goldfish, who would be soon scorched by the flames, their white bellies floating to the surface. But his worrying was in vain, for the goldfish continued swimming merrily through the water below the flames, unharmed.

But then a worry suddenly popped into Yasosuke's mind: *if the flames won't burn the goldfish, what will they burn?* An instant later the tips of the bright red flames turned and pointed towards Yasosuke, as if acknowledging his presence, and a powerful blast of hot air blew towards him.

"Aagghhhh!"

Yasosuke leapt back in surprise, and the flames persistently chased after him. He furiously tried to run away, but the flames relentlessly approached, coming closer and closer.

Yasosuke ran with such fervor that when he realized it, he was lying on the ground in a completely unfamiliar place. He looked back but could not see the flames anymore. There was no sign of the fire anywhere. All around him stretched endless darkness. The threat of the flames had passed, but in their place was an intense fear of the pitch dark, the fear of an interminable hell...

He tried turning his head to the side, but bumped into something hard. Yasosuke realized that he was lying face-up on the floor, at the bottom of hell. His head throbbed severely. Yasosuke extended a hand to his aching forehead, but his outstretched hand unexpectedly bumped into something hard at a level slightly above his chest.

What was the thing coming in contact with his finger in this place of complete, utter darkness?

Thump, thump.

(Oh...it's a board!)

The object touching Yasosuke's fingers felt like a board. But if it was a board, what was the board attached to? He stuck his hand straight up and groped around, but didn't make contact with anything. Next, he tried shifting his body slightly in one direction and reached up again. As he expected, something was there...

Thump, thump.

(Ah, there's also a board above me.)

There was a board on the side, above, and apparently below as well. He tried feeling around with his foot and discovered it truly was a board, which meant there must also be one directly above his head. But then what kind of place was he in? An enclosed space with boards on all sides...

"Oh, I know!"

Yasosuke's heart raced at a terrible speed.

"This is the inside of a coffin. I must be in a coffin!"

Yasosuke felt as if a massive rock was suddenly lowered onto his chest. He was now inside a coffin. But how did he manage to get inside it? He had finally felt the joy of being alive, woken from unconsciousness, but that joy disappeared after the briefest of moments. Being alive wasn't going to do him any good if he was stuck in a coffin. Even as the realization came to him that things were hopeless, he flapped his arms, legs, and head like a clockwork turtle. He knocked hard against the upper board. But as he knocked, another realization came to him.

(If I keep knocking like this, someone might discover me.)

Yasosuke imagined an altar somewhere upon which the coffin containing him was placed. But, given the fact there were no audible voices or sounds of a bell being rung, this theory was likely wrong.

(Then could I be in a morgue?)

If this was a morgue, then the silence was to be expected. Yes, this is probably a morgue, he thought. And so he stopped flailing about wildly and began to listen carefully, hoping to ascertain if any sounds were coming from outside.

"Oooh...I hear something!"

He was shocked, for there was clearly something there. It wasn't very loud, but sounded like the hissing of a faucet that had been left on.

"What is that hissing sound?"

A moment later, he heard a knocking sound. Then the high-pitched clang of metal against metal.

"What is this..."

It was a sound he had heard somewhere before. The knocking sound was quiet, but it shook Yasosuke to the core, like a powerful rumbling of the earth. He quieted his breath, remained still, and listened carefully to the strange sound.

Just when he realized a crackling sound had joined the other noises, Yasosuke's body began to grow mysteriously hot. Come to mention it—and this is something he should have realized earlier—ever since he had woken up in this pitch-black inside of a box it had been very warm, like a day in springtime. Given that it was now the middle of a harsh winter, this warmth was quite unusual. In any case, he had become fully aware of the unexpected rise in temperature because his body had suddenly become hot.

"What is happening?"

Just as he had this thought, the space before his eyes suddenly brightened. Having said that, it was no brighter than a few dim rays of light peeking up from the horizon at dawn. Oddly enough he didn't detect a foul odor—though later he would come to know this was because of having worn some kind of gas mask—but the combination of the light streaming in and the crackling sound of something burning had essentially brought upon him a hopeless despair. Because in his mind, the full nature of this mysterious place finally became evident.

"Aggh...I'm in a cremation oven! The fire has been lit and the coffin is starting to burn! Oh no, what's going to happen to me..."

Yasosuke began grinding together his teeth tightly.

Once-Seen Nightmare

Of all places, Yasosuke found himself inside the oven of a crematory.

(I'll be burned alive!)

Oh, what a horrific situation! Only moments after realizing he was alive, Yasosuke was threatened by being scorched alive in a fiery hell. Being burned after dying was one thing, but could there be a fate even crueler than being burned alive? Yasosuke visualized his arms and legs beginning to smolder and hair all over his body catching fire. He let slip a curse to nobody in particular.

"D-d-damnit..."

A snicker came from somewhere. A voice he was very...familiar with. It was *him*! That jerk Senshiro Nezumiya was laughing. Just then, as if on cue, the blaze flared up.

"You asshole! Fucking asshole!"

He desperately tried to move his immobile body. As a result, the twine tightly binding his body dug deeply into his flesh. Because of the sturdy twine, in a situation like this there was no way he would be able to tear it free from his wrists or snap it off his thighs. He wanted to get some part, any part of his body free. Then smash the boards of this coffin which was about to catch on fire...

"Aagghhh...Damnit..."

Covered in blood and sweat, Yasosuke roared and struggled like a wild animal.

But just then something happened.

He felt something unimaginable flowing towards him from the side. It seemed like an impossible miracle: a cool breeze gusting in from somewhere.

(What is this?)

Yasosuke halted his struggle for a moment.

(What happened?)

It seems that something just occurred.

His skin that was on the verge of being scorched suddenly felt cool.

The pain caused by the intense heat gradually began to abate.

(I think the fire has been extinguished!)

But the next instant, through the crack in the coffin's lid Yasosuke glimpsed a fire that was blazing even more fiercely. The oven was still burning furiously. And yet, inside the coffin Yasosuke's body had suddenly cooled down to a comfortable temperature.

Drip.

Something cold fell on to his chest.

"What the..." he began to scream out. But before he could finish, several drops of cold liquid came sprinkling down upon him.

"Oh, it's water...water is leaking out from somewhere."

In an instant, Yasosuke felt life returning to him. His mind calmed down. It looked like he was going to survive. Yasosuke rolled his eyes and looked all around, hoping to find something. There it was! Through the crack in the coffin was a bright red curtain of fire, and right in front of that, in a place that was probably very close to the coffin was a glass tube running diagonally through space. Inside the tube, a clear liquid mixed with tiny bubbles flowed by quickly. It must be water, coming from the same place as the water that just dripped upon his chest.

(How strange! A liquid cooling system within a crematory oven!)

Installing a mechanism for cooling in a place designed to burn bodies—what an odd idea! Just then he suddenly remembered that unusual dream.

"Goldfish were swimming in the water of a glass fishbowl...and on the water's surface was a curtain of flame...Yes, that's it!"

Like the goldfish swimming below flames, his own body was being carefully protected by a liquid cooling system.

"What are they trying to do to me?"

Yasosuke struggled to solve this mysterious riddle.

But just when he began to hear a creaking sound, the coffin around him started to, strangely enough, descend slowly as it swayed gently back and forth.

The Flying Coffin

Remaining mysteriously unharmed, the coffin containing Yasosuke gradually descended in the crematory's oven.

(What's happening?)

Amid Yasosuke's confusion the coffin suddenly stopped with a clunk, as if finally reaching the end of its descent. Before long there was a rumbling sound as the coffin began to slide sideways. It felt like the coffin had been loaded onto a truck and was being carried somewhere. Everything took place in utter darkness, but eventually another dim light appeared, looking not like sunlight, but electric light. Had he not been wearing a gas mask, Yasosuke would have likely detected the strong scent of earth, as if passing through a freshly dug underground tunnel.

Then Yasosuke heard a human voice whispering. He couldn't make out what was being said. Eventually the coffin moved as if carried on someone's shoulders and made a thud as it was loaded onto what seemed like a type of platform. A second later there was a hissing sound, and a burst of blue light could be seen through the crack in the coffin.

"Ha, ha, ha, ha..."

Laughing boomed outside of the coffin, as if mocking him. Yasosuke instinctively shrunk back in fear, but the next moment broke out into a cold sweat. Apparently an X-ray had been projected at him from outside the coffin. Using an X-ray, the insides of the coffin would be laid bare. It must be that the people outside saw him writhing around, like a skeleton dancing. Surely they were laughing because watching him struggling amused them.

"Hey, Yasosuke! Can you hear me?" said the hoarse voice of Senshiro.

Yasosuke was silent like a stone statue. But he was unable to calm his beating heart. In the end, he had no choice but to endure being ridiculed.

"...Of course you can hear me. Just hang in a little longer. Be strong!"

What is he talking about? Yasosuke felt a growing disgust.

(Fuck you asshole!)

Yasosuke abandoned all resistance and action, for he knew that struggling wouldn't get him anywhere. But the moment he gave in, exhaustion struck hard. With a rattle, the coffin began to sway again and was transferred to some other vehicle. There was a loud rumbling sound. Yasosuke was mesmerized, as if listening to a lullaby, and fell into a deep sleep. One moment the coffin was rising up lightly, only to fall again into the depths of hell with a thud. After everything that happened, the intense, repetitive jerking motion had no effect except to put him asleep, like a baby in a rocking crib.

After ten hours, or perhaps more like tens of hours, Yasosuke's coffin seemed to finally stop at its final destination. A great clamor suddenly erupted around him. A whistle rang out; music began to play; fireworks were launched. What exactly was going on here?

After passing through a terrible din that could be likened to a storm of cheering voices, in the end his coffin entered a room filled with dead silence.

Right then, a hushed voice once again approached the coffin.

"Well then, I guess I should finally let you out..."

"Yes, let me out!"

"Master Ichinomiya, may I begin the procedures?"

"Yes, go ahead..."

There was the sound of a rope being undone, and then a clanging noise, like nails being removed. It was finally time to leave this coffin. But where had Yasosuke ended up? Also, "Master Ichinomiya" sounded like a name he had heard somewhere before, Yasosuke thought as he shook his head repeatedly inside the coffin.

Crematoria

For the rest of his life, Yasosuke thought he would never forget the strange feelings and the amazement he felt when the lid of the coffin—it did turn out to be a coffin after all—was finally opened. But what was even more bizarre, truly bizarre, was the world outside of the coffin.

Before him stood several men and women. Yasosuke recognized two of the men. It goes without saying that one was Senshiro Nezumiya, the mysterious praying-mantis man who had brought him all the way here. But who was that other guy?

(That's a face I've seen before...)

Yasosuke made a quick effort to remember the man's name, but it remained hidden on the edge of his consciousness on the verge of recall. The man was extremely tall, with a chubby red face, and beneath his nose was a striking mustache of around ten centimeters long.

For some reason the entire room, everything from the ceiling and the walls to the furniture, was painted in a grayish-green. On the center of one wall was a large glass window. The window seemed to be situated at a very high altitude and looked out over an expansive ocean. The visible land mass below was a burnt brown color. Around the coast was a steep precipice going straight down to the ocean. On one area of the land, a portion of a massive building was visible. The structure was nothing like the usual perfectly square buildings formed from straight lines that we are all accustomed to, but was instead shaped with organic-looking curves. Furthermore, there was something unspeakably eerie about the building that gave Yasosuke chills from even a quick glance. It was the same brown color, except for the tip of what looked like a tower tinged in a blood-red color. That too had a mysterious power to it, making his heart race in a disturbing way.

(Where in the world am I?)

It didn't seem like Japan. And yet, Yasosuke didn't feel as if he had traveled very far from Japan.

"So, are you awake?" said the chubby man with the beautiful white mustache.

"Oh..." said Yasosuke and looked at the man's face. But as he was gazing at the face whose healthy complexion was reminiscent of a sausage, he suddenly screamed out in shock, having finally realized the answer to a question that had been on his mind.

"Kono, I have someone to introduce to you," said Senshiro without hesitation after he stepped out from the crowd and approached Yasosuke.

"This is the honorable General Ichinomiya."

"I knew it was him!"

Speaking of General Ichinomiya, wasn't that the general who had regrettably passed away, and was now on black-bordered display in a window in the Shinjuku night market? Come to mention it, he was famous for his beautiful mustache. Indeed, that very same mustache was on the elderly gentleman standing here.

"But General Ichinomiya was supposed to have passed away..."

"Ha, ha, ha!" the general looked up as he laughed, belly shaking vigorously. "I died and came here, you see. Just like Senshiro here, and you yourself who have just arrived."

"No, I didn't die. I have no memory of dying."

"You might have a memory of *not* dying, but there's no way you'd have a memory of dying. But anyway, it's only because you died that you were able to be inside that thing over there, that coffin."

Yasosuke glanced towards where the general pointed and saw the coffin that had contained him for all this time, tossed disorderly into a corner of the room.

"Oh, that means...that means this is the underworld, right?"

"Not quite."

"What do you mean?"

The general gazed for a few moments at Yasosuke's puzzled expression, then opened his mouth quietly.

"This place is, in other words...the nation of Crematoria."

A Bizarre Tale

"Crematoria?"

A look of confusion on his face, Yasosuke yelled out the word said by this man who called himself General Ichinomiya.

"That's right. Isn't the name 'Crematoria' self-explanatory?" said the general before turning his head to the side. "What do you think, Senshiro? Would you mind explaining a little about this country to him? After all, you know more than anyone about this place."

"Yes sir. Well then, shall I give him a real shock?" said Senshiro as he shot Yasosuke a penetrating glance.

"But before that, there's something I must say," continued Senshiro.

(Oh no, here it comes...)

"Now that we have brought you here, I want you to refrain from ever going back to Japan, no matter what happens. To begin with, your funeral has already taken place, where you were officially pronounced dead. Even if you return to Japan, just as you mistook me as a ghost, you'll have no way to prevent everyone there from being terrified, thinking you are a ghost too."

"Did you say my funeral has already happened?"

"That's right. You should remember that day when we drank together in a Shinjuku bar and you passed out. That was the effect of the potent narcotic I slipped into your drink that put you into a near-dead state. Even a doctor would probably examine you and say you were truly dead. After collapsing, you were taken temporarily back to your apartment and were then given a funeral, with all your relatives attending. Even your parents and friends were present, and everyone believes that your body was cremated at the Hanayama Crematory."

"That's impossible..."

"Your family received an urn full of ashes and returned home with it, without suspecting a thing."

"But then those ashes are..."

"Of course, those are the ashes from some horse, or a random person. You probably don't know this, but in this day and age anyone can get hold of human ashes if they need to."

"H-how could you...you horrible fraud of a cremator!"

"Yes, I am indeed a fraud of a cremator. I'm sure you remember the days of my youth...I was not the type of person with so little confidence in my abilities that I would be content with ill fortune. In other words, I became a head cremator because of an important goal I had in mind. Can you guess why I became a cremator?"

Yasosuke said nothing. By this point he had a pretty good guess, but knowing this man was not in his right mind he couldn't just tell him out straight. It was best to stay quiet.

"I desired to make possible what seemed impossible and create a wonderful, carefree society. Have you ever experienced when New Year's Eve rolls around, and everything feels somehow relaxed and carefree? When there are only two or three days left in the year and you realize that no matter how much you rush to get things done, it's out of your hands...it's that feeling that makes those last few days of the year feel completely relaxed and carefree. So what happens if you take this to the furthest extent? You end up removing yourself completely from everyday society, as if you no longer existed."

"Hmm," Yasosuke grumbled.

"Essentially, you create your own death certificate and join the ranks of the deceased. By doing that, you can cut ties with all the unpleasant things in this world. You'll no longer have the debt collector at your door, nor will you have to care for a bunch of children; when you grow old, you won't have to worry about others mocking your senility. Once you are officially dead, you can live out the rest of your life however you desire, in complete freedom. Can there be anything more enjoyable than this? That's the idea that gave birth to this great country of Crematoria."

Senshiro's hideous cheeks flushed a deep red.

Returning to White Smoke

Senshiro's soliloquy continued.

"After working in the Hanayama Crematory for a long time, I hit upon the idea of creating a special mechanism in the cremation oven. Essentially, faux cremation. No matter who was watching, as long as a coffin was tossed into the oven and things properly sealed, they would have faith in the result. But what was actually sealed was only the front-facing surface. The other surfaces—the left, right, top, bottom, and back walls—were all made to look like solid walls of fireproof brick. Nobody would ever consider doing a detailed examination of those five walls. Taking advantage of that, I created a mechanism which, after sealing and closing the front opening, would use a specially made cooling system to prevent the coffin from being consumed by the fire. Next, I designed a system that would lower the coffin down into a hidden underground room, directly below the oven. Finally, I sprinkled ashes and human bones that I had prepared in advance on the brick floor of the oven. That did it. The bereaved never suspected a thing."

"You fiend! You must have taken my wife's body and set her free in the same way."

"Just hold on for a second...Once I succeeded in creating these mechanisms, next I made a breakthrough that involved putting human beings into a near-dead state. This is a truly amazing discovery. It requires quite an unusual drug; colorless and tasteless once dissolved in water, and no one will realize it is there. When someone unknowingly swallows it, they will be put into a coma and eventually a state of near-death. Furthermore, in this ingenious condition even a doctor will be forced to diagnose the person as being clinically dead. These two inventions gave me the power to create the utopia that is Crematoria. As for everyone who is here now, all those deemed to be a good fit were covertly put into a near-death state, sent to Crematoria on an airplane, and then resuscitated in this room in the same way you just were. I promise to you that I will bring everyone here that is deserving, whether it is a man of distinguished ability or a young and beautiful woman. My request to General Ichinomiya, now standing before us, was because I thought he would be the most appropriate to lead the construction of Crematoria. He sympathized with my cause and invested his entire fortune in this country."

"Then where is this place? It can't be Japan."

"You're correct. It's an uninhabited island, south of the Ogasawara islands."

"What happened to my wife Tsuyuko. Bring me to her immediately!"

"Oh, Tsuyuko?" Senshiro said, his expression darkening.

"I don't mind letting you see her, but before that you must make me a promise."

"Promise?"

"Once you become a resident of Crematoria, I'd like you to become the head of the department of literature."

"Department of literature?"

"Yes. I'd like you to use your literary talents to develop the literature of this country."

"You are asking me to...*develop your literature?*"

The moment Yasosuke heard the word "literature" he suddenly came to his senses. Yes, even if his writing didn't sell, his soul was deeply connected to literature. But it was because he wrote using inspiration from his experiences in a bustling city that his work had a certain passion to it. This was a utopia, yet any writing inspired by an uninhabited island, no matter how you look at it, would be dry, tasteless, and uninteresting. Not to mention that no detective story would ever emerge from a utopia such as this. He felt a longing, even a sense of pride about being a third-rate author forever wandering the city's backstreets. Realizing this, he felt acute homesickness suddenly strike him, like an arrow directly in the heart.

"I would like to decline your offer. I'm returning to Tokyo."

"What do you mean 'returning to Tokyo'?...Don't you want to see Tsuyuko?"

"That's right. I suddenly have a strong desire to go home. I have no intention of indulging in your far-fetched ideas of happiness. Hanging around that cluttered city of Tokyo as a writer who has lost his wife suits me best. I'm leaving."

"So you are saying you're leaving, no matter what?" said Senshiro with a touch of sadness in his voice.

"Yes, I'm going home!"

"Well, in that case, I have no choice," he said, gritting his teeth tightly as he took a few steps back.

Bang.

A gunshot rang out. Pure white smoke expanded in front of Yasosuke's nose, and that was the end of him...Consequently, our story of Crematoria too must come to an end.

EIGHTEEN O'CLOCK MUSIC BATH

Chapter 1

In the wake of the sun, twilight fell upon the Earth.

At the edge of encroaching dusk, the 18 o'clock time signal solemnly commanded the hearts of His nation's one million citizens.

"Oh, it's 18 o'clock!"

"Time for the 18 o'clock music bath."

"All right everyone, quickly take your seats and don't be late!"

In Alishia District, there were only three: Professor Kohak and the college students Penn and Bara. They had opened the door and darted into the blue hallway an instant before hearing the time signal.

A row of seats stretched far down the hallway, each made from a thick, silvery luminescent metal pipe bent into a spiral.

Each person jumped into the chair bearing their name. As if on cue, three round, yellow windows opened in the ceiling and released sprays of yellow onto the figures below. Delightfully refreshing sprays.

The three waited in silence for the music bath to begin.

Professor Kohak was a middle-aged man clothed in the same color as his long, inky black hair, combed back messily as if he'd hastily run his fingers through it. A slender build complimented his above-average height. His features had a graceful quality to them, yet at the same time gave the impression of a passion bubbling quietly, but vigorously beneath his slightly pale skin. Elbows resting on knees, the professor sat deeply in his spiral chair, as if deep in thought. At times, his eyelids would jerk back and forth in their sockets, perhaps because the eyeballs beneath were writhing in agony.

Penn was young, a similar age to Bara. He extended his hand towards Bara sitting beside him, moving slowly to avoid being caught, and touched her plump backside.

Slap.

Bara's reprimand needed no words.

The back of Penn's hand was red and swollen. Still, it continued to plead, to seduce.

"Only two more hours," Bara's hand whispered softly to Penn's hand.

But Penn's hand persisted.

"I may be gone before two hours is up. So please darling, just for this moment..."

"Shh! The warning signal was just given."

A voice burst from the loudspeaker: *One person is missing in the neighboring Alishiro District.*

As if part of a prearranged sequence, they each turned to look to the right, towards Alishiro District. Just then the door opened and a man darted into the hallway. In a fluster, he hopped frog-like into his seat.

"Oh, it's Paul," Penn said with a chuckle.

"That scrap battery is probably doing dissections on his own again. What an indecent man!" Bara said and spat in disgust.

A purple light flooded the length of the hallway.

Professor Kohak slowly raised his head.

"All right, the music bath is starting. Now raise your hands..." the professor advised his two students.

Just as three pairs of hands went up, the music began: a barely audible groan emanating from somewhere deep in the earth.

"Shoot, it's that terrible soul-stealing #39!" Penn cursed to himself.

Transmitted through the spiral chairs, National Melody #39 progressively intensified. The professor stared dumbly into space; Bara's eyes were closed, lips twitching; Penn gritted his teeth together tightly below a profusely sweating forehead.

The National Melody continued its slow build, cooking the citizens' brainstems like scalding steam. Moans akin to wild beasts emerged from various places along the long, purple-tinged hallway, and the wall reverberated violently as if fired upon by a cannon.

Behold, the purple purgatory!

The music bath progressed amid the citizens' sticky sweat and wailing voices. Thirty minutes later, the purple rays of light began to weaken little by little, until at last a refreshing spray rained down through the yellow, circular windows onto their heads, just like in the beginning.

The music bath was over.

As if roused from a nightmare, the citizens in their spiral chairs gazed up at the ceiling and looked around vacantly.

"Ugh...the music bath is over."

"All right, let's get out of here. There's a mountain of fabric waiting for us back at the factory."

"Yeah, we should make up for that schedule slippage yesterday."

The citizens, bursting with energy, hopped out of their spiral chairs.

With a spring in their step and a renewed vigor nothing like their former selves, Penn and Bara followed after the lively Professor Kohak and returned to Alishia District.

Chapter 2

The call had come from Aloaa District.

Professor Kohak walked over and pressed the button on the receiver. A momentary ripple in its mirror-like surface quickly became President Miluki's face, buried in a thick beard.

"President Miluki, long live the empire!" the professor said in greeting.

"Ah, Professor, I have a matter to discuss with you in private." The beard wiggled as he spoke.

The professor acknowledged this and turned around, ordering Penn and Bara to the adjacent workshop.

The students each grabbed two handfuls of papers from the desk, pushed open the door, and escaped to the next room.

"I am alone now. What would this be about?"

"Well, the fact of the matter is that I would like to express my respect for you, professor. Thanks to the tremendous power of your music bath, this nation is under my complete control. At the end of each bath, it is as if each and every one of my citizens has been reborn. Each and every person burns with the same ideals of this nation and is ready to apply themselves fully to their duties with an equal passion. They do my bidding without exception, just like androids. Even the most brutal, dangerous criminal is transformed into a model citizen after a thirty-minute music bath. Each of my people is in perfect health. And I have you, professor, to thank for these wonderful citizens. You have my deepest respect..."

"Your Excellency, might I respectfully ask that you get to the point."

"Ah, yes." The beard swayed. "Well then, I am aware that at present you are researching the construction of androids, but I think that perhaps it would be best if you halted that project."

"So you mean to order me to cease the android research? Might I ask why?"

"To put it plainly: can you not see that, thanks to the 18 o'clock music bath, my citizens have obtained minds and bodies of steel? Each of them has become an ideal human being. Given that, is there truly a need to create androids? The cost of the android research has risen to half of the national budget. Why must we spend such a vast sum of money on this project? What I mean is that with our music bath system in place, there is no need for androids. Professor, how do you feel about this matter?"

"I understand what Your Excellency is saying. Please permit me to think things over."

"Yes, you do that—oh, I nearly forgot. My wife apparently wants to see you. Can you stop by for a little while this evening?"

"Yes, Your Excellency. I will pay her a visit at 20 o'clock tonight."

In the workshop next door, Penn and Bara earnestly continued their calculations. They were so involved in their work they had no awareness of each other's presence. Even here, the effect of the music bath was tremendous. In this nation, the hour immediately following the music bath was the most precious; the most important tasks were all undertaken in this short time period, with superhuman ability. The national defense shield, nutritional provisions, mixed bacteria—each of these was improved or redesigned during this hour. Once it was over, everyone either pursued work that didn't require creativity, played, or slept. While the 18 o'clock music bath turned the entire populace into geniuses for an hour, it also forced them to follow the nation's sound ideals for the remaining 23 hours. The music bath was based on the earth-shaking vibrational music of the Central Music Plant, channeled to human brains through spiral-shaped chairs, massaging brain cells and transforming each citizen into a uniformly outstanding, standardized subject. In recent times, the music bath has utilized National Melody #39, a melody skillfully refined over many iterations by the professor at President Miluki's request, designed for the purpose of creating so-called "Type 39 Standard Subjects." Type 39 Standard Subjects were those who fulfilled some 39 conditions identified by the president as necessary for his citizens.

An exhaustive list of all 39 conditions will be omitted here, but to point out a few: to be loyal to the president, to possess an unyielding spirit, to not want after alcohol, to not smoke, to maintain good health through four hours of sleep, and to recognize the president immediately upon seeing his beard. President Miluki had given out some very forbidding conditions.

When Professor Kohak completed National Melody #39, the president was ecstatic. The song was experimentally tested on the nation's worst felon who was promptly reformed into a model citizen, exactly as President Miluki had desired, so it was only natural for him to be shocked so terribly that he nearly passed out. Thus the president ordered the successful music bath to be left playing over the radio waves, exposing the citizens to it 24 hours a day. However, this idea was rejected by Professor Kohak; he objected on the grounds that the music bath unnaturally stimulates brain cells and overexposure will destroy them, leading to sudden death. Hence, current regulations limit the music bath to only thirty minutes a day, as per the professor's guidance. The president, if given such an opportunity, nonetheless wished to extend the time in order to completely capture the souls of the populace. He had just expressed to the professor his joy at having such perfect citizens, but that was nothing more than an empty compliment. In reality, the people were in a continual state of tension throughout the day, far from living complaint-free.

Chapter 3

The time was sometime after 19 o'clock.

Speaking of 19 o'clock, this time corresponds with what used to be called "7 p.m." in the old manner of expressing time. In this underground nation the people lived under constant artificial lighting, with no true dawn or dusk; but the sun's languid rays continued to shine down upon the Earth's surface, serving as the roof of the entire nation. Not even a butterfly flew above the surface. As a result of repeated wars, bacteria and poisonous gas had caused great ruin, resulting in a place of great desolation, devoid of life and unable to support even a single blade of grass. The surviving humans, along with a small number of livestock and parasitic organisms, managed to escape underground and preserve their species.

Now returning to the matter of what happened after 19 o'clock: Penn from Alishia District and Paul, a shoemaker of Alishiro, engaged in a heated discussion as they licked the inside of a honey jar in a private room.

"Come on, don't you think this is completely ridiculous?"

Paul gestured largely as he spoke, trying his best to convince Penn.

"Well, yes," said Penn, a hint of confusion on his face.

"That's all you have to say, Penn? Our freedom is being taken from us, our individuality ignored. As human beings, we want to smoke tobacco. We want to drink alcohol. But His Excellency the Asshole won't let us drink or smoke. What do we have to live for anymore?"

"Hey, please keep your voice down! It won't be good if someone hears us."

"Jeez, give me a break. If somebody does hear us I'm sure they'd agree completely. Anybody who doesn't is a poor sap, still under the influence of that abominable Melody #39."

"By the way, Paul, it seems like the president's beloved music bath isn't having much of an effect on you."

"Of course it's not!" Paul said brazenly, puffing up his chest. "What I'm about to tell you is in the strictest confidence. Now, touch my backside for a moment."

Eyes shining with curiosity, Penn did as he was told and touched the back of Paul's pants. There he felt something with a rough texture, like a bamboo cage.

"Oh my, what is this? What did you put in there?"

Paul laughed. "You know what I did? This, you see, is a *vibration attenuator* that I created over a year using strengthened fibers. As you know, only a small part of that music bath comes in through the ears; most of it comes from the ground, entering the body through those spiral chairs. By simply putting the vibration attenuator into my pants like this, I can significantly reduce the vibrations of Melody #39 being transmitted through the spiral chair. That's why that soul-eating music can't get to me."

"Hmm, interesting. You're certainly a man who toys with danger. But what if you're discovered?"

"If I'm discovered I'll know you blabbed. Now listen up. If you keep quiet, I'll never be discovered. I'm quite skilled at groaning to pretend that my soul is being devoured by that music. I even sweat profusely. You probably didn't know this, but there are microphones hidden in the front of the seats; all of our groaning voices are transmitted to the Department of the Prime Minister's observation room. All of your groans are clearly monitored on a self-recording readout. If you forget to groan, an alarm will go off. I would never make *that* kind of mistake."

The disgusted look on Penn's face grew more pronounced by the moment. He was shocked that one of his close friends was a man who was shamelessly pulling one over on President Miluki—the lord of the underworld, judge of good and evil. Behind every formidable government was an equally formidable opposition. Penn realized that Paul wasn't the only participant in this crime. While speaking to Paul, he felt the anesthetic effect of the music bath gradually wear off; Penn felt that he himself, like Paul, was a blasphemer of President Miluki.

"Hey Paul. You'd better be careful about Bara. She was making a big fuss about how you were a scrap battery. If she gets wind of your big secret, it's not going to be pretty."

"Penn, Bara is your wife. As long as you don't screw up, there's no fear of her finding out."

"Yeah, but that woman is as shrewd as any man. I can't tell her what to do."

"Penn, for a husband you sure whine miserably."

"Actually, I'm considering giving up being a husband. Being married to a woman like that completely sucks the life out of me."

"Really, are you serious? If you got divorced I'm sure you'd just find another wife. Do you have someone in mind?"

"Are you kidding? There aren't any nice girls out there who are right for me. Hey Paul, to be honest...I think it would be great if you weren't my guy friend, but my *girl* friend."

"*Girl* friend?" Paul blinked his eyes, mouth agape. "Penn, do you really mean that?"

"Do I mean it? Of course I do. Why would you ask that sort of thing?"

Paul grabbed Penn's hand and silently led him behind a dividing partition in the corner of the room.

There was the sound of clothes shuffling. Paul's shirt appeared, draped over the top of the partition. There was a clang as a belt was drooped over the partition.

At that moment, a startled yell came from behind the partition; Penn's screams drowned out the voice of Paul trying to calm him down.

"Oh...That's what she meant by the rumor you were doing dissections on your own body. That is some serious surgery you've done. You disgust me!"

Chapter 4

It was exactly 20 o'clock, as promised.

A lone figure stood before a door in Aloaa District—a tall, neatly dressed man.

"Lady Miluki" read the nameplate on the door.

The door slid silently down into the ground.

Inside was a wall of pure white satin. A beautiful woman stood before it, evoking a relief sculpture; from the neck down she wore equally white, skin-tight clothes of satin— or perhaps we should call it a new type of underwear with connected top and bottom, extending to the wrists and ankles, underneath a loose, translucent gown made from infinitesimally thin, flexible glass that glowed brightly as it trailed behind her.

"Ah, Professor Kohak, I presume."

The man kneeled down reverently upon hearing Lady Miluki's pure, bell-like voice.

"I pledge my loyalty to you, My Lady."

Lady Miluki laughed daintily and led the professor into a room. Inside was a dazzling array of decorations, checkered in gold and red from ceiling to floor. Expensive crystalware cluttered a large glass table in the center of the room; a lavish dinner had been prepared in advance. Lady Miluki motioned for the professor to sit in a chair across from her.

In the middle of the glass table was an object shaped like a tall bookcase. Lady Miluki pressed a button and a conveyor belt within began to move vertically in the fashion of an elevator. Various items such as aged liquors and delicious-looking dishes emerged quietly from below the table and were mechanically placed before them. Used dishes were automatically lowered below the table, disappearing from sight. When the lady raised a glass of vintage 1937 wine, the professor immediately raised his own glass as an instinctual reaction; when she grabbed some hornet larvae and raised them to her mouth, he followed suit. They conversed in the pauses between bites.

"Professor, the music bath you have designed has produced amazing results. President Miluki himself is exceedingly pleased. You have my greatest respect."

The professor bowed his head and remained silent.

"But, having said that..." she said, pausing to put down her wine glass. "The contributions of your music bath are tremendous, and yet I cannot help but be concerned by the equally tremendous problems it is causing."

The professor froze, moving only his mouth in response. "Problems?"

"The music bath is an affront to the people's humanity. National Melody #39 was created based only on the conditions of a self-serving ruler. People are altered to be prone to mental manipulation, yet there is no consideration given to whether it is reasonable to perform such alteration on an actual human being. Indeed, thanks to the music bath the nation's people have improved incredibly in many areas, including their physical condition, productivity, and even conduct. But on the other hand, forsaking their humanity is causing a toxic buildup of discontent within their bodies. As this accumulates day and night, things will inevitably reach a breaking point in the near future. I sense that a subset of the populace has already come to realize this toxic buildup of discontent."

"Even assuming there was some sort of discontent accumulating, shouldn't the 18 o'clock music bath be eliminating that?"

"It only appears to be. Perhaps it does eliminate it for a time, but it does not eliminate it completely. An anesthetic is, after all, only an anesthetic. There is no way someone as wise as you would not realize this."

"Lady Miluki, I am but a scientist who has sworn allegiance to the president, and I act only in accordance with his orders."

"I implore you, be silent. You claim to be nothing but a scientist who invents things such as an android or a music bath. But why, oh why, are you *only* a scientist? You could be a far better politician. You are such a distinguished figure that even the president is no match for you."

"You greatly exaggerate, my lady. I am simply a citizen who has pledged allegiance to the president, a man who strives to follow orders faithfully."

"That cannot be. You cannot imagine how much better off this country would be if you were in control instead of Miluki. If you were our ruler, I myself would be *unmeasurably* happier. Now professor, face me and look into my eyes. Behold my quivering lips. You are the only man in this world to whom I can entrust my body and soul. Oh professor, I beseech you to hold me, to command me. I will do anything for you. As Miluki's beautiful wife, if I speak even a single word before the people, they will obey. If I declare that you, Professor Kohak, are the only one whom I truly love and respect, and order the nation to swear loyalty to you, I am certain that all million citizens will immediately comply. Come, let us build a better nation together. Let us build a new nation where we put above all else the people's desires: love, lust, and personal choice. Professor, hold me now!"

Lady Miluki twisted her supple body in the likeness of a reptile as she stood up from her chair, and threw herself directly onto Professor Kohak's lap.

Chapter 5

"Oh professor, is there something wrong with you?" Lady Miluki raised her voice in concern from the professor's lap.

The professor continued staring wordlessly into space.

"Why, your body is as cold as a corpse! I feel chilled, as atop a block of ice. Oh, how terribly unpleasant! I question whether you are even a living being."

The professor giggled. "I seem to be dead and yet living at the same time!"

"Pardon, could you repeat that?" she said, clinging to the professor's chest, but just then the door burst open and a group of people clamored into the room. Among them was President Miluki and the wiry-haired secretary of state, Madam Asari.

In the blink of an eye Lady Miluki jumped off the professor. President Miluki, large eyes bulging out from within his beard, shook his fist like a steel ball as he approached the professor.

"What a wondorous scene we have here...Since the laws prohibit sexual relations between a commoner and the president's wife, I never expected to see such a sight. I don't know whether you were aware of this, but this horrendous scene of blasphemy has been broadcast live to the entire country. It is not just I who has witnessed this, but the entire nation. I presume both of you are fully aware of the consequences of your actions."

The professor seemed completely unfazed.

"Assuming that there was a TV broadcast sent nationwide, everything I said in this room must have been heard and understood by everyone. That undoubtedly proves my innocence."

Madam Asari then stepped out from behind the president, her face red with hatred.

"Professor, it's a real pity, but only your actions were visible on the TV broadcast. As the audio transmission was shut off, not even a peep came from the loudspeakers. That's why I doubt even a single citizen knows what you were saying."

"What? Broadcasting only our images, but not our voices—you ask me to believe such a ridiculous thing? With all due respect Your Excellency, current regulations mandate that TV broadcasts shall be accompanied by audio."

Professor Kohak's sudden burst of eloquence was a drastic change from only moments ago.

The secretary of state laughed impudently. "The laws are decided by the president. Hypothetically, if today he were to amend the law to no longer require TV and audio to be broadcast together, your objection would no longer hold water. Am I wrong? That's why I am honored to respectfully declare that such an amendment was just enacted today. No longer is it illegal to broadcast TV on its own—"

"I will not permit such deception! This is a depraved plot to fabricate a romantic relationship between the lady and I. Why this slander? Why this fraud? Please explain at once."

Standing erect, Professor Kohak spat out the words as if breathing fire.

Color quickly drained from the president's bearded face. But he still gave the order, voice quivering.

"All this talk is pointless. Secretary Asari, you will have them executed as I had previously decreed. Immediately!"

After issuing this declaration he stormed outside the room following after Madam Asari, closing the door behind him.

Lady Miluki, her back to the wall as she quietly watched this exchange, tried to dart from the room herself in shock at what just happened. But the door, like a wall of solid steel, refused to move even the slightest bit.

"Please open the door! What are you trying to do to me? President, this isn't how things were supposed to happen!"

Lady Miluki pounded the door frantically. She pressed the button next to the door again and again, but the door still showed no sign of movement.

Just then, a hissing sound, like gas leaking from a pipe, came from somewhere in the room.

The lady was the first to discern the sound. She began wringing her own neck with lithe, lipstick-red fingers.

"Oh my, it's poison gas! Why would you ever kill *me*? Ugh...please open the...open the door."

With a quiet hiss, the light grey poison gas gathered low on the ground, swirling like mist, then inched higher and higher. The area around Lady Miluki's windpipe soon darkened to a deep crimson. Her fingers reddened. The tiny red droplets splattered even onto the white silk on her chest. Face pale, the lady's breath rasped violently like a bellows.

Professor Kohak stood unmoving like a clay figure within the grayish gas, completely oblivious to the lady writhing in agony beside him. He appeared to be lost in thought.

Suddenly, he began moving, running around the room in circles like a squirrel searching for something on the four surrounding walls.

Thanks to a TV receiver, the room's interior could be clearly seen from outside. On the wall-mounted receiver Lady Miluki could be seen suffering in agony. Professor Kohak continued running in circles like a madman.

Staring intently into the TV receiver were President Miluki and Secretary of State Madam Asari. They watched the events unfold inside the room with a burning interest.

But before long, they realized something was wrong: the professor's face now filled the TV receiver's screen. The lens of the transmitter had been found at last. The next instant, just as the professor raised a chair over his head, the screen flashed and the image went dead.

Standing before the receiver they took turns spinning dials, but not even a blip appeared on the screen. The device that had been capturing the room's interior had been completely destroyed. President Miluki and the wiry-haired Madam Asari locked eyes.

"We can't see anything. What should we do?"

"There is no longer any need to watch. Clearly, they will both will die in there."

"I'm not too sure of that, madam."

"I have no doubt of it."

Right as she said this, a deafening roar bellowed from the direction of Lady Miluki's room.

Miluki exclaimed in surprise, covering his ears. "What is going on over there?"

"President, let's quickly go see what happened. The professor may have broken down the door and escaped."

But the door was still firmly in place. After talking it over, they decided to attempt opening the door. An electrician standing guard switched on the power so the door came down smoothly when they pressed the button.

They dashed into the room. It looked like a great explosion had occurred, with nothing left of the luxurious decorations, only a terrible state of ruin that was painful on the eyes. Legs and arms were scattered about in pieces on the floor. When the secretary stepped into the room to pick up one of the limbs, a flame suddenly enveloped the floor with a *whoosh* as if in wait of their arrival. Even Madam Asari—normally a strong, brave woman—stood petrified, lost at what to do in such a situation. The pieces of body parts strewn upon the floor disappeared into the flames.

The bodies of Lady Miluki and Professor Kohak were assumed to have turned to smoke, by now drifting through Aloaa District. But the source of the blast was never found. The only possibility that came to mind was that the professor had carried it in himself. As to why he would have prepared an explosive and ignited it, killing himself in the process, President Miluki couldn't find a satisfying answer to this.

Chapter 6

Never in a thousand years could Penn and Bara have guessed the terrible fate that had befallen Professor Kohak.

Bara exchanged offensive jokes with Penn in her private room. But before long, their excitement fizzled out like a typhoon breaking up a cloud of mist. In the midst of their boredom they found themselves sighing lazily.

They both wondered why things felt so dull.

"These days you've been rather aloof," said Penn.

"Look who's talking? Don't blame me," Bara said, gently rubbing the caress doll that lay beside her pillow. The caress doll was a popular item used to stimulate the sense of touch through rubbing, recently discovered as an alternative pleasure to smoking (the latter now being prohibited by law).

"You've grown tired of me, haven't you?"

"Well, I don't know...I just feel so irritated lately. I can't put my finger on it, but it's like there's some lingering doubt building within me, day by day. I have this strong feeling I'm about to fall mentally ill because my body can't take it anymore."

"Now that you mention it, I can't say I don't feel the same way. So basically you're sick of me and have fallen in love with someone else."

"Oh no, that's not it at all. Maybe it's not only you that I'm tired of, but everyone."

"If you're tired of everyone, you're done for. I'm not like that, although I won't claim I don't hate anyone. Earlier today, I told Paul that he disgusted me. He really is an indecent man. You were right."

"Right about what?"

"You said he was dissecting his own body, didn't you?"

"Seriously? You mean *that* rumor?"

"That's right. Paul did surgery on his own body. That's why he disgusts me. Keep this between us, but he's trying to change his gender."

"What?! Change his gender? Oh, maybe he...yes, tell me more."

"There's not much to tell...isn't it obvious? That guy has done surgery to cease being a man and has nearly completed the transition to a woman."

"Seriously? Is that sort of thing even possible?"

"Possible? He's practically achieved his goal. How disgusting! This terrible situation is all because of advances in VHF surgery that have made performing surgery on the human body easy, just like making a sculpture."

"In an age where even androids can be made, of course we can do something like that. But a living being changing his or her own gender, that takes some serious determination. What a wonderful idea!"

For some reason, Bara suddenly got out of bed and, with an air of excitement, pounded her flat chest with her bulky arms.

"What's wrong with you? Why are you acting like that?" Pen yelled, frowning.

"Oh, he's done such a wonderful thing. Paul really outdid himself; that man is too good to be a shoemaker. Now that you mention it, I'm not surprised what he did. After all, for us oppressed citizens it's the only escape, or shall I say the only way of rebelling against the government. With smoking prohibited, drinking banned, and that soul-wrenching 18 o'clock music bath, what freedoms do we have left? Thanks to advances in medicine, we have obtained eternal life and preservation of youth. Death only happens as a result of capital punishment or suicides, the latter requiring exceptional ingenuity to pull off. There is no need to give birth to children, except when a special order is given by the government. When someone is given the death penalty, the government selects a woman to be artificially inseminated, she becomes pregnant with a single baby and is admitted into the National Hospital of Reproduction to give birth to a new person, replenishing the lost one. In ancient times the purpose of sexual desire was for procreation, but in the modern age we know only sexual desire for its own sake. In Miluki Nation we have had every possible liberty taken from us—save a newfound sexual independence and freedom. And yet, until now we have not known how to enjoy that freedom in any real sense. Paul is indeed a wise man, the true hero of this nation. He has made sex into a sport and devised a way to escape from the yoke of gender, all in order to liberate humanity and pave the way to a new world of freedom. No longer must I remain a woman for my entire life. I can become a man. If I changed from a woman to a man, I wonder if you would feel the same about me."

Overpowered by Bara's impassioned tirade, Penn was dumbfounded. He sighed and parted his trembling lips to speak.

"You becoming a man, what a horrific notion! This relationship is over. It's now painfully clear to me there's yet another thing to make my life miserable."

Chapter 7

On account of an emergency call from Secretary of State Madam Asari, students Penn and Bara had to leave the room immediately. They had received word that the secretary and President Miluki would be visiting Alishia District in five minutes.

The pair adeptly transferred to the express conveyor road and made it back to Alishia District just in time. "I don't see Professor Kohak. I wonder what happened to him."

"Hmm, I'm not sure. It's the appointed time and he's not here. How strange."

They immediately noticed the professor's absence. Fearing President Miluki's wrath, they called all manner of people and searched each room, but there was no sign of the professor anywhere.

"You searched inside the laboratory closet and under the desk too, right?" Penn asked.

"Of course. I did everything I could, but I couldn't find him anywhere. Nobody seems to know either."

"Nobody? Who did you ask?"

"Who?" Bara laughed, "I asked everyone."

For some reason Bara's frown became an awkward smile.

Shortly after, they heard an uproar outside that they took to be the secretary's arrival.

They both rushed to the door.

"Oh, it's..."

"Oh my, the president is..."

They had expected the secretary to arrive by herself, yet to their great surprise she escorted the president, who now stood there arrogantly.

Madam Asari barged into the room, casting a scornful look at Penn and Bara. Then she turned away (though not towards anyone in particular) and began to speak.

"Professor Kohak of Alishia District has been executed today as punishment for his part in the scandalous incident involving Lady Miluki. Therefore, for the time being, I, Secretary Asari, will take charge of that district, concurrent with my existing post. Additionally, Bara is hereby ordered to become provisional vice head. That is all."

Penn and Bara began to tremble hysterically as if electrocuted; this was the first they had heard of the professor's violent death.

It was hard to believe that anything scandalous could have occurred between Professor Kohak and Lady Miluki. The professor had shut himself up in the laboratory and devoted nearly all 24 hours of the day to his work. He wouldn't have had the time or the motivation to get involved in such a thing. But if he did, what exactly would it entail? Besides, Professor Kohak was the nation's number one—or more accurately the nation's star scientist. He was Miluki Nation's most valuable treasure. Under direction from President Miluki, the professor had designed and built a variety of cultural facilities. Executing him amounted to an act of suicide for the nation. Who was going to continue the professor's work with him gone? What a terribly thoughtless death sentence. Furthermore, what would become of the androids that had been in development, having already consumed an enormous portion of the national budget? The professor's two pupils felt as if the ground had suddenly caved in before their eyes to form a several-kilometer gorge.

"And thus, Vice Head Madam Bara, I hereby order you to accompany the president on an inspection of the entire Alishia District where Professor Kohak had been assigned. You will depart for your assignment immediately."

Bara felt a tinge of joy at being called vice head, though she had no desire to lead the president through Alishia District.

But an order was an order. She had no choice but to begin guiding President Miluki's party through each room, beginning with the next workshop.

The entire Alishia District was on a single floor, with a total of sixteen rooms in various sizes. But the only one intimately familiar with all sixteen rooms was Professor Kohak. Bara knew of nine of them, and Penn only six. All citizens from the same district were legally permitted to have knowledge of every inch of that area, but the professor had broken convention and restricted access to the laboratory based on position.

The inspection of the first six rooms completed without any difficulty. To be sure, they found some unusual things, but nothing particularly shocking. Then Bara turned to face the crowd and spoke. "Beginning with the seventh room are laboratories mainly focused on secret android research. We will be coming across some strange sights now, so please be prepared..." she said, not forgetting to warn them.

They entered the seventh room, where, sure enough, there was a great number of large-scale power machinery standing together like trees in a forest. Each contained a nuclear decomposition engine powered by artificial cosmic rays. The units were organized into twenty-four hubs, each further branching off into numerous power distribution wires that were fed through transformers. One wall of the room was covered with bundles of these wires, a sight resembling a piece of knitted fabric viewed under a microscope. The complete absence of sound gave the impression of being on the bottom of the ocean, making the room that much more disturbing.

They entered the eighth room where reference specimens were stored, a place perhaps best called a museum of automata. All manner of man-made automata were put on display, beginning with items from the 4th century BC. Approximately 700 models were present: marionette-like contraptions and armored warriors, progressing to radio-controlled units built with relays, and remarkably human-like models with artificial skin. These specimens of automata gazed eternally at the ceiling with eerie expressions, tightly crowded like a hall of mummies, stiff shoulder to stiff shoulder.

Penn stared wide-eyed as he wrung his hands, clearly made uncomfortable by the strangeness of these rooms he was seeing for the first time.

"Now this is the ninth room. Things *will* get a little noisy here," Bara said in the manner of a tour guide.

President Miluki and the secretary exchanged anxious glances, but a moment later they thrust out their chests and elbows, trying to act tough in front of the door to the ninth room.

Despite having promised to guide the party, for some reason Bara hesitated awkwardly to open the door. Secretary Asari quickly picked up on this and got hysterical, as she was apt to do.

"Open the door this instant! Dawdling here will not do us any good," Madam Asari said as she glared at Bara.

Still, Bara's hesitation continued; she even withdrew her handkerchief frequently and dabbed sweat from her forehead. Penn grew concerned when he saw Bara's behavior and backed away from the door.

The secretary's face gradually reddened as rage bubbled up inside her.

"So you aren't going to open it. Well if you aren't, I will. But you'd best prepare to be punished."

Just as the secretary tried to push open the door, Bara leaped in front of it.

"That...that's dangerous. Please stop. If you open the door now, it will explode."

Chapter 8

Hearing the word "explode" sent a chill down Madam Asari's spine; it had triggered her memory of when they had tried to cruelly murder the professor in Lady Miluki's room and there was an unexpected explosion, tearing off both of their limbs and scattering the pieces everywhere. "Well then, we have no choice. I will open the door after engaging the fail-safe."

Her face devoid of fear as if accepting her fate, Bara began twiddling three dials in front of the door. Three pilot lights blinked in succession: green, red, then yellow. Soon the door began to open silently inwards. The group fearfully peered inside the room through the slowly widening gap.

"The ninth room is where the professor had stored his prototypes. Please refrain from teasing the creatures inside."

Bara leading the way, they cautiously entered the room.

The group was shocked by the very first thing they laid their eyes on: of all things, a naked woman stood there, surveying their faces in a glance.

She looked approximately 17 or 18 years of age, boasting a beautiful body of pure, glossy white, which called to mind frozen milk. But, more than anything, it was her charming face that caught their eyes; search the world and you'll never find a girl quite as good looking. Something about her was reminiscent of Venus de Milo, but perhaps it would be better to say she more closely resembled an angel. Not particularly embarrassed about her body (which literally lacked even a shred of clothing) she smiled at the group.

"What a beauty!" President Miluki cried out shamelessly with a lascivious joy. "What's her name?"

"She has been given the name Annette," answered Bara on behalf of the young girl.

"Oh, so her name is Annette. That's a really nice name, but I think it would be better to give her a name that is simpler and suits her better."

"But Your Excellency, you mustn't misunderstand. Annette is an android. Please take a close look at her body."

"What? Look at her body?"

President Miluki opened his eyes wide like saucers and slowly looked over Annette's body.

"Ah, I see."

When the president looked down he couldn't help but smile, for he had discovered a part of her body that was incomplete, very different from that of a real human.

"Well then, please allow me to explain. What you see living in this room are all experimental creatures made by Professor Kohak. This four-legged thing that looks like a piglet has an artificial heart and body, and a brain transplanted from a German shepherd. Next, we have a monkey with the brain of a human child..."

Standing before the wire cages, Bara described the creatures one by one.

It was a collection of incredibly strange creatures; there wasn't an ordinary one in the bunch. Some looked human. There was the top half of a man, soaking in a large glass container filled with a yellow liquid. He held a glass tube to his mouth with both hands and continually sipped a purple liquid. Tracing the tube to its origin, there was an elaborate chemical apparatus attached, but at the input to the apparatus the liquid inside the tube was yellow. Essentially, a cycle was formed by a yellow liquid being transformed to a purple liquid, and then back to yellow as it passed through the half-body. Bara explained that it was a new experiment focused on studying nutritional intake.

Even during Bara's explanations President Miluki seemed anxious, distracted by the android Annette. Secretary Madam Asari didn't fail to take notice of the president's demeanor, and because of that her face gradually paled as her body trembled.

However, President Miluki did not seem to pay any attention to the madam's reaction and instead separated from the group, returning to where Annette was standing.

"Lovely Annette, what are you doing here?"

Annette smiled broadly like a deranged mute woman.

"Oh, Your Excellency," Bara approached the president with a look of concern. "Annette is a prototype, so she only understands a special set of codes. She doesn't know the Milukian Language."

"What? She doesn't understand Milukian? How terribly inconvenient," he said. But the president's attraction only grew stronger toward Annette, who perhaps should be called a crazed beauty.

Just then, the secretary gritted her teeth together tightly as if struggling to restrain herself, then ran over to Annette's side. Face drained of color, the secretary withdrew a knife from an inner breast pocket with a flash, and, holding it like an icepick, moved her arm to thrust it straight into Annette's heart. But at the last moment Bara jumped on Madam Asari's arm, risking her own life, and just managed to prevent harm to the android. But the secretary was in a frenzy, and Bara herself was extremely worked up.

"Secretary, what are you doing?"

"That's none of your business! I have the authority to kill this android and I will!"

"Please refrain from killing her."

"Why are you interfering? It may be wrong to kill a living human being, but what is so wicked about killing a mechanical android? Just looking at this good-for-nothing woman makes me sick to my stomach. By my authority, I *will* kill Annette."

"No, no—you must not kill Annette! In the several weeks since her construction, she has looked after the prototypes in this room. She has spoken with us and we have become friends. Annette is no different than a real person. Killing her is just...absurd!"

Bara held tightly to the secretary's arm that gripped the knife and refused to let go.

"So, you wish to oppose the secretary of state. Well then, you will not be forgiven!"

"But, please Madam Asari, I beg you to reconsider...and another thing, we should protect the ones that remain, because if the professor is gone we may never be able to build androids again. That would be the worst possible loss for Miluki Nation!"

"The worst possible loss? How presumptuous of you," Madam Asari chuckled. "I suppose you have fallen in love with this android."

Bara was silent.

The secretary grabbed hold of Bara's hair and in a fit of rage tried to drag her down to the floor. President Miluki, shocked by this, roared out.

"Wait, Madam Asari. By the name of Miluki, I prohibit you from causing harm to this android! These androids are a precious product of our nation's research. Over time I've spent 80 billion Rukul on this research. You cannot kill these androids. Now put away the knife."

"Your Excellency," Madam Asari said as she grabbed the president by his collar. "I will obey your order. But promise me this: you must never speak to these good-for-nothing androids like they are real people."

"Yes, I know that. And you know more than anyone that I have no ulterior motives here."

With that, the secretary's eyes suddenly narrowed as she blushed in embarrassment.

In the corner Penn stood alone, disgusted by what had happened.

"Oh, how very unpleasant. Bara has fallen in love with an android, and the secretary is having an affair with President Miluki. With all this going on, there was really no reason for me to hold back. My good friend Paul the shoemaker altered his body to become a woman, but he surely did it in order to be with me. All right, I think I'll go and settle things with Paul now."

Chapter 9

The next morning, President Miluki and Secretary Asari were having breakfast together.

Even though the secretary was wearing pajamas, the president had on regular clothes.

"Your Excellency, I am aware that you slipped out late last night. You can't keep it secret from me. Where were you?"

"No, I just, well you see..."

"There's no use trying to hide things from me. One of my men just told me he had spotted you around Alishia District."

"You're saying someone saw *me* in Alishia District?" President Miluki said, eyes wide.

"On what business did you go through all the trouble to get out of bed in the middle of the night?"

"Business? Oh, it was nothing special...It seems like you have some misunderstanding, and I don't like it. Yesterday we discovered something in Alishia District, did we not?"

"Discovered what?"

"Well, we discovered that basically...um, what was that again...yesterday we went to check out Alishia District but could only see up to the ninth room. There was all that fuss about how if we tried to forcibly open the door leading to rooms ten and beyond, it would explode. But not being able to enter those rooms was proof of the unpleasant fact that there exist places in this nation where my absolute power does not extend to. In light of that extremely unfortunate fact I went there to investigate whether there was any way to get inside."

"My, aren't you courageous lately? So were you able to get inside of the tenth room as you had hoped?"

147

"No, I failed."

"You should have known that from the start. Anyway, why were you in Alishia District until morning?"

"Come now, I was simply doing my best to try and get the door open."

"Yes, of course. But I don't know what door you were actually trying to open."

Madam Asari turned towards a blue parrot on a nearby metal perch and held out her fork, a piece of meat stuck on its tip.

With blinding speed the hungry bird opened its beak and snapped up the meat. But a moment later there was the sound of something falling to the floor. The hungry parrot had dropped the precious piece of meat on the ground, without the slightest hesitation.

"Here now, Pinto," the president called the bird's name. "Are you not feeling well?"

Thereupon Madam Asari answered on behalf of the parrot. "No, Pinto is in perfect health. He's just saying that the disgusting android meat doesn't suit his taste."

"Did you just say *android meat*?"

President Miluki jumped up from his chair, shocked. He turned his gaze to Madam Asari's feet where there was a heaping pile of red meat chunks in a large metal dish. The president, a disturbed look on his face, caught sight of a trail of blood drops leading from the dish to somewhere behind the inner curtains.

"You did this, didn't you!"

President Miluki rushed frantically over to the curtain and on its far side discovered a pile of intricate machine parts dismantled. On the edge of the pile was the beautiful face of a woman. Though slightly discolored, it maintained a bright smile as if nothing had happened. Seeing this, the president immediately burst into a rage like a volcano erupting.

"W-why did you kill her? Why did you kill Annette? Yes, you must have been jealous of her beauty, you bitch. I had given you a strict order to not kill the androids, which you blatantly disobeyed. Secretary or not, you will never be forgiven for this!"

Madam Asari sat down, calmly sipped her beverage from the glass, and then spoke.

"Now, will you please hush? I did this with the best interests of this nation in mind. Can you imagine what great chaos would ensue if the populace learned that the president was obsessed with an android, especially at an important time like this? As I have said before, now is the time to take emergency measures. I am certain that Your Wise Excellency understands that."

The president did not refute Madam Asari's claims. He just turned away and mumbled quietly to himself.

"I am nothing but a prisoner in a cell without bars, but a cell nonetheless. I am now doomed to an eternity without a beautiful woman..."

Madam Asari feigned ignorance of the president's mumbling. Eventually she sat him down at the table as before and began to patiently discuss national strategy.

"Now then, President Miluki. Beginning today, our nation is going to carry out emergency maneuvers."

"Emergency maneuvers, indeed. So what exactly do you suggest?"

"There is an unlimited supply of gold buried beneath our nation. We will mine that up within a week's time."

"Who is going to mine it? Mining all that in only a week...First of all, we lack the manpower, nor do we have enough machines."

"That's no excuse. Leave everything to me."

"Leave it to you?" the president sniffed disdainfully. "It's glaringly obvious that your plan will fail. If only Professor Kohak was still alive, I'm certain he'd succeed magnificently. You may be a politician, but you're no scientist."

"Scientists are only necessary in the beginning. After things develop to this point, execution is all that remains. And skillfully executing a large undertaking requires none other than politicians. Science can never dominate government, but government will invariably dominate science."

"I myself felt that way, at least until yesterday. After meeting Annette the android, I began to doubt whether it was true. Oh, beautiful Annette...In the depths of the tenth room of Alishia District, there may be hundreds, even thousands of androids even more beautiful than her. The power of science is incomparable!"

"Gold reigns over science. I will unearth the gold beneath us in a week and rebuild this nation with it: gold roads, gold rooms, gold ceilings, gold walls—everything gold. What a wonderful plan, don't you think? Our nation will rule the world with gold!"

"Rule the world? That requires iron, not gold. Gold cannot win a war."

"I disagree. With enough gold, there will be any number of countries offering to defend our nation with iron. All that is needed is to invite the prime minister of a country who tries to start a war to our nation and promise them a room built from pure gold, and wars will be a thing of the past."

"I doubt whether it will be that simple. I'm not nearly the optimist you are."

In the middle of their conversation, they heard a delicate sound in the distance—a melody they had heard many times before. The music bath had begun.

"The music bath? It's the 18 o'clock music bath," the president said and blinked his eyes in surprise. "Hold on a minute. It's 8 o'clock now. The music bath has started in error. What is the person in charge doing?"

Madam Asari, her demeanor free of panic, spoke to President Miluki like she was reprimanding a small child.

"Yes, it is the music bath. I've changed the music bath regulations beginning today. From now on it will occur every other hour, twelve times in a day. By doing this, the people will get nearly twelve times as much work done. Sleeping and eating will no longer be necessary. After experiencing the music bath, the people will be stimulated enough to work for an hour and a half without rest, just like carriage horses. After that, we will simply give them another music bath."

"That's absolutely reckless. The late Professor Kohak would never try such a thing."

"Professor Kohak was a cunning fellow by nature, which is why he purposefully limited the music bath to once a day. Otherwise, he too would be forced to work around the clock. I've known that for quite some time now. Only a true politician can actually increase a country's productivity in any real sense. It takes politicians in control to bring out the true power of science."

At that moment, President Miluki heard his citizens' gasps of anguish ringing crystal-clear in his ears, escalating as the music bath progressed.

Chapter 10

President Miluki paced noisily around the room, his sullen mood a drastic change from the previous day.

Sitting before the electric makeup table, the secretary massaged her secretory glands repeatedly with radio waves as she persistently spoke with the president.

"Your Excellency, in time you will thank me. You may not be aware of this, but there has been a recent rise in unspeakable, vile acts once the effects of the music bath have worn off and the people grow bored—questionable sex experiments, men becoming women, and women men. With all this going on there's no telling how dejected their spirits will become. Your Excellency is far too lenient on them. It's an utter waste of time to allow them time to sleep, eat, think, or play.

"Such things will only cause boredom and serve no purpose, except to lead them astray. This recent trend of depraved behavior is proof of that. For that reason, I have expanded the music bath to occur every other hour, not just to redeem this country but to redeem its people. If we still fail to see sufficient effect, I would like to enact what I consider the ideal music bath: 24 hours a day, without stopping. Only then can we command the entire nation as a single unit with everyone moving in lockstep."

"That will rob them of every last bit of freedom. There's surely no need to go that far."

"I disagree. My plan will also immeasurably improve the people's well being, for it will eliminate all of their worries for good."

"I object to this!"

"Your Excellency, with all due respect you only feel that way because you lack the aptitude to be a politician. Now you must do as I say—entrust me, a born politician, with the full responsibility for governing this country. Then you will resign. This will put your mind completely at peace."

"Don't be an idiot. That would be treason. I am the eternal ruler of this nation. I will never relinquish it to you!"

The secretary laughed scornfully. "No matter what you say, I have you and this nation in the palm of my hand. It is now I who is the brains of the nation. You have no choice but to grant me full power."

She jutted out her high-cheekboned face and roared shamelessly with laughter.

President Miluki stomped in frustration, realizing finally that he had lost both his beloved, the beautiful Lady Miluki and the wise, venerable Professor Kohak, all because of the secretary's plot. But dwelling on misfortune was pointless. It also struck the president that he had been reduced to the level of Madam Asari's plaything.

Around thirty minutes later the emergency alarm suddenly went off, shaking the foundations of Miluki Nation. So what could have happened?

The people gathered before the loudspeakers in unison, faces pale from worry as they listened to the alarm blaring out, loud to some and soft to others. A message came in from Hoshimi, the head of the Division of Astronomy.

"Warning! This is a public announcement from the Division of Astronomy. At 8 o'clock and 40 minutes a member of our staff observed an unusual rocket ship 10 degrees southeast from the North Star, and follow-up observations of the rocket ship in question have determined it to be on a direct collision course with Miluki Nation. Furthermore, the time of arrival has been estimated to be 23 o'clock, the day after tomorrow."

A rocket from Mars! An attack from the Martians had been postulated for several centuries. The time of the dreaded attack had finally come.

By the way, apparently some radio wave signal, unknown to the Bureau of Transmission, has been strongly interfering with their receivers in the last ten days. It must have been a signal coming from the Martian rocket. The Division of Astronomy had just now detected the rocket on their electronic telescope.

"If the Martians were to come," Professor Kohak had once declared, "it would not be with peaceful intentions." His fears had manifested now as an undeniable fact that could not be ignored. What might be the purpose of this attack? The people of Miluki Nation thought it was because of the inexhaustible layer of gold buried beneath them. No matter the era, those who yearn for riches must someday sacrifice themselves for those same riches.

Faced with an urgent national crisis, out of necessity the conflict between Secretary Madam Asari and President Miluki naturally resolved itself.

"Your Excellency, I feel that the negligence of the Division of Astronomy, who failed to detect the arrival of the Mars rocket arriving the day after tomorrow, must be severely reprimanded."

"We can consider that at a later time. More importantly, we should have them observe what type of weapons that rocket ship is equipped with and report that information to us."

As they were talking, a report from the Division of Astronomy came in via the speaking tube. It was the voice of Division Head Hoshimi.

"—any further observation will be extremely difficult. Yes, that's right."

"What is going on over there? I am beginning to doubt your patriotism."

"No, Madam Asari, that is not the problem. The entire staff is burning with patriotism, it's just they are over-excited. They are trying to manipulate their instruments, but not a single person can calm down enough to make precise observations. They are only operating at half of their normal efficiency."

"How weak humans are! Well then, why don't you do the observations yourself?"

"I'm no different than the others. It's as if my brain is somehow numb."

"In that case, I guess we should start the music bath again."

"No Madam, that's not going to work. It's the music bath that doing the numbing."

"Damn it, I refuse to listen to any more excuses! The moment you or your staff don't fulfill their duties, I'm dispatching the executioner."

"Madam Asari, if you are going to give me the death penalty as you did with Professor Kohak, you might as well do so now. I'd be better off dying as opposed to seeing myself degenerate further."

"Silence, Hoshimi. As of now you are dismissed from your post as head and will be imprisoned. I appoint your assistant Runami as the new head of the division."

"Oh, Runami? That poor thing won't be able to handle the job."

"Why? Why would that be?"

"Runami, a man with a weak mind and body, has gone completely crazy from the music bath. Not only has he stopped making observations, he is running around berserk, breaking any valuable equipment he can get his hands on with a wrench, all while singing the national anthem at the top of his lungs. Unable to endure the music bath, that poor man has lost his mind."

"That's impossible...I'm going to go see for myself immediately. You're just trying to scare me with your lies."

The call ended there.

Madam Asari began getting dressed.

President Miluki approached Asari from behind with a look of concern. "I can't have you rushing off to the Division of Astronomy now. If we don't give orders at once to the bombing and reconnaissance squadrons to deal with the rocket ship and prepare for combat, it will be too late."

Madam Asari puffed out her cheeks in defiance. But she still halted her preparations to go out and quickly made a TV phone call to the reconnaissance and bombing squadron leaders.

However, there was no sign of either of them on the receiver screen, just an empty square wall.

"What's happened to them?" President Miluki asked.

"Nothing. It's just that the 10 o'clock music bath is beginning right now."

Indeed, the music bath's melody could be heard softly in the distance. In accordance with the music bath regulations, the two squad leaders stepped out into the hallway and were sitting in their respective seats. Face distorted with rage, President Miluki spoke.

"Damn it. That's just not acceptable. You honestly had them cease their battle preparations and have a music bath instead? Having every member of this nation leave their posts and sit in a music bath—that's absolutely absurd!"

"I beg to differ. If we don't do this, we will never be able to freely manipulate them."

"If the Martian rocket ship starts firing poison gas shells at us, do you expect us to politely request for them to wait for our nation's music bath to be finished?"

President Miluki was livid.

Chapter 11

An announcement declared the music bath to be over. The secretary quickly summoned the reconnaissance and bombing squadron leaders to the TV phone. Their faces appeared on the screen, practically mirror images of each other: large, googly eyes and emaciated cheeks, wheezing like asthma patients. The secretary was shocked; she had never seen them this haggard before.

The squadron leaders were given strict orders to begin mobilization and prepare for combat. They respectfully accepted the orders, gaunt faces aglow with loyalty. The secretary was utterly delighted, her dejection and anger forgotten in an instant.

"What do you think, Your Excellency? I have never seen those two tremble with such deep emotion."

"I'm not too sure about that...Personally, I can no longer stand to look at the faces of my people."

"Your Excellency, you are so easily affected by such things. Don't worry, just leave it to those two loyal leaders and everything will be fine."

After only four or five minutes passed, the bell of the TV phone rang and the faces of the two squadron leaders appeared once again on the screen. The exhaustion on their faces was unmistakable. It was as if they had aged five or six years in this short period of time.

The two leaders expressed how they had issued an emergency summons to the soldiers and then called roll. But they went on to give a shocking report of what happened next. "...Despite the soldiers' high spirits, they were all in poor health, without a single individual suitable for combat."

At first, the secretary couldn't believe this. But after thoroughly questioning them she had no choice but to grudgingly accept the truth: every soldier had been severely affected by the music bath. Some were driven mad, or nearly so; others lost a fifth of their body weight in only a day's time or even fell ill from acute disease to their vital organs. The result was a state of complete annihilation for both the reconnaissance and bombing squadrons (whose duty it was to drive back the enemy and protect the nation), despite not having actually engaged into combat. Miluki Nation had essentially committed suicide. In under three hours, the secretary's 24-hour music bath regulation had unleashed terrible devastation on the nation. The only two people still sitting comfortably were the chubby Madam Asari and President Miluki, who had no obligation to be exposed to the music bath.

During this entire time, announcements continued from the Division of Astronomy in a feeble voice about the approaching Martian rocket ship.

"What has happened to this nation..." said President Miluki, no longer making any effort to conceal his despair. The squadron leader answered from within the screen.

"Of course, at this rate the Martian rocket ship will have no trouble infiltrating Miluki Nation. If we had only one hundred strong soldiers, we could prevent the capital from falling, at least for a time. Even fifty soldiers might make a difference, but my squadron is currently...Agghhh!"

The secretary, listening to this, twitched an eyebrow as if finally making up her mind about something.

"Aha, the last resort!" she screamed suddenly.

"The last resort?"

"Yes, the last resort. Breaking down Alishia District's inner door and getting a hold of the androids hidden there by Professor Kohak. Then we deploy them into combat."

"Of course, the androids!" President Miluki said as he clapped his hands, though the look of concern promptly returned to his face. "But is there truly a collection of strong robots like that in Alishia District? Besides, that door just won't budge. The word is that it will explode if forced open."

"Well, we haven't confirmed that yet, but I do have a feeling it's true. I'm going to open that door, sacrificing whatever is needed."

"Sacrificing whatever is needed?" said the squadron leader with a frown. Right then the secretary, trembling in anticipation in the middle of the room, suddenly gave a resolute order.

"I command the bombing squadron to advance to Alishia District and destroy the door there at once. The reconnaissance squadron is to wait in reserve for further orders."

On the screen, the two squadron leaders' faces stiffened, like fish taken out of the water. President Miluki moaned and threw himself onto the sofa dramatically.

Back in Alishia District, Penn and Bara looked nothing like their former selves, their skin-and-bone bodies resembling mummies.

Penn was drawing a diagram of some incomprehensible device on his drafting board, drenched by a constant flow of drool from his lips. Bara, now a bone fide man, worked noisily on a calculator, continuing a reckless effort to perform the division of an indivisible number down to several billion decimal places; at times, he would randomly call the name of his beloved Annette as if delirious from fever.

The bombing squadron suddenly barged into Alishia District (now looking like a gloomy mental institution), and the large group of weary, over-exhausted soldiers poured in like a mudslide. Shocked, Penn and Bara clung to the walls like bats.

On a signal from the leader, they began the work of destroying the door to the tenth room. A job that normally took a single person now required over twenty people. One after another, soldiers died pitifully gripping the oxyhydrogen cutting torch. Even the smallest exertion put a sudden stop to their weary hearts.

In her private room, the secretary's mood quickly deteriorated as she digested the reports coming in moment by moment. Corpses continued to pile up outside the tenth door, and when she heard that not only could the door not be opened, but the dead bodies could no longer be carried away, Madam Asari gave the order for the reconnaissance squadron on standby to advance.

But what can one expect from soldiers who were like a cluster of seriously ill families?

Nevertheless, the door was finally destroyed. But once the heroes of the reconnaissance squadron saw that beyond the door was another resilient door, they fell onto their asses like a bundle of rice plants toppled by the wind.

The secretary organized the national army and ordered them to move out. After that, the secondary and tertiary national squadrons were dispatched to assist. Still, the entrance to the tenth room didn't budge.

The national anthem was played continuously in order to encourage the troops, but having exceeded their maximum dosage of stimulation the only thing it encouraged was an unproductive loss of consciousness. In the end, the only two members of Miluki Nation with any strength left were President Miluki and Madam Asari.

Even so, the secretary made no attempt to give the order to cease attacking. She was like a woman possessed.

They finally exited the room and advanced down the hallway towards Alishia District. For the first time they were baptized by the music bath, a very pleasing sensation. But as time went on, their brains were gradually cooked by the fast-paced music; a nausea-inducing, unpleasant feeling slowly crept up on them. They practically tumbled into the entrance of Alishia District.

Echoing, blood-curdling screams of the dead. Piles upon piles of corpses. They looked around in horror. Deeper in, a closed door seemed to taunt them.

"Shall we?" asked President Miluki.

"All right, let's go," responded Madam Asari.

"Let's charge the door."

"OK, here we go..."

It appeared that even they themselves did not know their objective in charging the door. Burning with the passion of martyrs, the last surviving members of Miluki Nation rushed headlong towards the steel door, following their self-assigned orders.

At that moment, there was a sensation of their bodies being enveloped by yellow sparks. That was the end. They lost consciousness as if tossed from a precipice—and in the blink of an eye the room fell into the deep silence of a centuries-old graveyard.

But if someone were to listen carefully, they would hear a strange grating sound, like something was being dragged deep within the earth. Transmitted through the thick walls, the sound gradually intensified as if something was rising up from below. Moments later came a metallic clang, and the iron door of the tenth room—which, up to now, had seemed to have a massive immovable stone affixed to it— began gradually, soundlessly, to open inward. Who could be opening the door?

Who was on the other side of that door?

The figure who calmly appeared on the other side of the open door to the tenth room was none other than Professor Kohak, a man long assumed dead. A strange beetle-like suit of armor covered his body. Behind the professor, roughly 500 androids resembling Annette accompanied him in silence.

The professor turned the first dial attached to his suit. A faint red flame arced between his shoulders as electricity was discharged; the distant melody of the nation's music bath suddenly halted, as if a switch had been flipped.

The professor now adjusted the second dial. The army of robots standing in the back walked past him in a well-formed line towards the front of the room. Two of the robots stayed behind in place of Penn and Bara. Each android took up an important post to replace a lost citizen of Miluki Nation.

Professor Kohak then turned the third dial.

In response a soft, pleasant melody began to play.

Shortly after, an android's face appeared on the room's TV phone. The face turned towards the professor and began speaking.

"The song that had been decreed by law has been completely destroyed. In its place, a hymn to mankind has begun."

The professor nodded quietly. A music bath to extol a new humanity! Would the massive piles of corpses be reborn by this new music bath?

But the dead bodies, now cold like tombstones, remained motionless.

The professor entered the command room and, using the massive control panel inside, skillfully manipulated 500 soulless androids.

Great shrieks rang out as electric cannons fired heavy shells in succession towards the Martian rocket ship, all at the hands of androids.

Several hundred attack ships rose from the surface in a beeline towards the sky. Underground, mountains of artillery shells, poison gas shells, and demagnetizing shells were manufactured, all at the hands of androids.

The professor listened peacefully, entranced by the melody of this new music bath, a hymn extolling humanity.

A song for humanity. Was it played for the citizens of Miluki Nation, the frigid corpses? Or was it played to transplant human souls into the professor's beautiful androids? No, it was a requiem, played for the sole surviving human, Professor Kohak, who now wielded absolute power. To the professor, a man of outstanding intelligence, reviving Miluki Nation's heaps of corpses was not a particularly difficult undertaking. But he didn't have the slightest intention of doing so. Scientists are, in the end, a cold-hearted bunch.

In truth, Professor Kohak had done all this in order to construct his long-cherished utopia, with firm conviction and great confidence. After becoming privy to the secretary's plot, he had fashioned an android in his likeness and sent it to explode in President Miluki's room. This was for two reasons: to set the stage for today's events, and to cover up the android's existence.

Immersed in the new music bath, an anthem for a new humanity, the emergent Android Nation of Kohak took the first step towards the establishment of a new world.

ABOUT THE AUTHOR

Sano Shoichi, writing under the pseudonym Juza Unno, was active from the late 1920s to the late 1940s, and has been referred to as the founding father of Japanese science fiction. Familiar with the western SF of his time (he translated works from the classic authors Jules Verne and Arthur Conan Doyle into Japanese), Juza Unno was a prolific writer whose stories skillfully integrate many imaginative topics such as outer space, aliens, teleportation, and robots—all at a time before the genre of science fiction was popular. He studied electrical engineering at Waseda university, and the accuracy of the scientific and technological elements in his stories attest to his technical knowledge.

His works would later influence generations of Japanese authors and manga artists. For example, Osamu Tezuka, creator of the classic manga *Astro Boy,* specifically mentioned the influence of Unno in one of his essay collections. In Tezuka's unfinished manga series *Phoenix,* a character is put into a hibernation-like state, an element similar to Juza Unno's story *The World in One Thousand Years.* The first name of a character in the classic 1974 anime *Space Battleship Yamato* was named after Unno (Juzo Okita).

Juza Unno's works cover a wide range of topics and genres beyond SF including mystery, dystopia, adventure, and even poems. His stories often have twists to them that illustrate the dark side technology can have when misused.

www.ingramcontent.com/pod-product-compliance
Lightning Source LLC
Chambersburg PA
CBHW022129170626
46808CB00002B/905